Nola -
enjoy
We hope to see you again
one of these days! Jody

Missing in Central Standard Time

Jody Vorbrich

Jody Vorbrich
2015

Shooting Star Publishing

Missing in Central Standard Time

Cover Design: Craig White, WhiteInk Design & Illustration
Text Design and Layout: Susan White

Cover Photos: Ellen Nolan Photography
Author Photo: Ellen Nolan Photography

Printed in USA by 48HrBooks (www.48HrBooks.com)

For Peter, Jill, and Jason

Acknowledgements

It's always nice (no, it's wonderful) when that very first manuscript reader says, "I loved it. It's better than your first." Before I hear those words, I always think, "Oh no, she must not like it at all because I haven't heard from her." In this case, that first reader was Jan Clayton and I owe her my gratitude for taking the time to read "Missing in Central Standard Time" with her critical, sleuth eye for the cozy mystery genre.

The people who helped me in the writing of this book are Fred Scaletta, Public Information Officer for Iowa Penal System; Mark Schlenker for legal information; Jim Travis, Iowa Department of Corrections for information on search and rescue dogs; Bob and Annie Leonard, Knoxville, for their support; my local chapter of Sisters in Crime for their support and friendship; Patty Ciechanowski and Ellen Wobbeking for police procedural information; and Jackie Saunders, a talented writer herself, who improved every chapter with her fine eye for detail.

I also thank many friends who helped and advised me: Audrey Venenga who has actually visited someone in prison;

Mary Kay Shanley who continues to be my mentor and gives me praise I do not deserve; my writing group (Sherry Borzo, Dory Briles, Nawal Ghali, Melanie Hewitt, Scarlett Lunning Huey, Carol McGarvey, Kathy Quinn, and Sandy Smith, with special thanks to Kathy Meyer and Margaret Ann Comito for their thoughtful suggestions); Kay Barber for all things Las Vegas-related; and to my recipe donors Sharon Huff for her sweet and salty pecan recipe; Michele Yannuzzi for her pizzelle recipe; Ellen Wobbeking for her lemon bars; and Kara Berrie for her cutout cookie recipe.

My invaluable editor, Mary Jo Graham, deserves special recognition for her deft editorial touch and also for helping me with the publishing process. She believed in me from the very first chapter of my first book and encouraged me to continue writing.

A big thanks to my brother, Bill Nolan, who knows all about horses and straightened me out several times, and to my great-niece, Ellen Nolan, for taking my photo with Toad on the coldest day of winter.

And last but not least, I couldn't have written both *Murder in Central Standard Time* and *Missing in Central Standard Time* without the support of Lynn Vorbrich, otherwise known to me as husband extraordinaire.

"There is in every true woman's heart a spark of heavenly fire, which lies dormant in the broad daylight of prosperity; but which kindles up, and beams and blazes in the dark hour of adversity."

—Washington Irving

Preface

I wanted to tell Deputy Al to stop calling me "ma'am," but a dog was barking and people were running in its direction. Al took off toward the field with me behind him. We slipped and slid all the way, tripping over snow-buried weeds and rocks. Men in parkas and a barking dog were cloistered around a lump on the ground among the corn stalks. I could only make out brown fabric before Al turned around and suggested I get back to my car.

"Please, Mary Jo, we'll do this by the book and that does not include having a civilian witness this. Go on now. Bobby wouldn't want you here. You know that."

I backed up and turned to go. Al was right. I didn't belong here. It reminded me of last spring when I found myself trapped in a barn with a madwoman. I cringed and hauled myself back up to my car where I stood with Kevin for a few minutes. Then a woman, who I guessed to be Hannah DeGroot, came running out the front door of the house with no coat or boots on—just faded jeans, a plaid flannel shirt and tennies. I took off running trying to catch up with her, but couldn't. We both reached the commotion at the same time. Corn stalks lay stamped flat in the snow. The circle of men parted, and there it was. I saw ribs and hoped it was just a deer injured on the road who found a quiet place to die. Then, I saw the faded blue overalls frozen to the corpse. One arm absent of flesh stretched outward. I didn't see the face but imagined there was not much left to see.

Hannah started crying. Then we both were pulled away, but not before Hannah screamed something I couldn't make out. It sounded like, "He looks human. He looks human." She kept screaming it. Al took her arm, and she went somewhat willingly with him back to the house. The cadaver dog's trainer led it away, hopefully, for a "good job" treat. I followed Al and Hannah up the incline toward the house. She had to be freezing, and Al urged her on. Another deputy caught up with them. Al told him to call for an ambulance and notify the county coroner's office. Then he added, "He might want to meet the ambulance at the morgue. Get the state troopers to send a technician and a crime scene van. I'll be inside with Hannah. Can you wait for them in your car and show them the body when they get here?"

Al turned to me and smiled. "Good eye, Mary Jo. Noticing their corn hadn't been picked, I mean. Can you take Kevin home for me, or better yet, is he supposed to work today? That would be good for him, I think. To be with you at the Nook."

I nodded sure, and looked to the house. An old witch's face stared out at me from a dirty window pane. It scared me more than seeing the bones in the field. I turned and headed for my car.

Before I left, two TV news trucks pulled into the farm lane and stopped before they got to the house. I shouldn't have been surprised. Holland is a small community, and Des Moines is less than an hour away. I grabbed Kevin who was waiting at my car. He looked pale but assured me he was okay.

However, that was four days ago. Let me begin at the beginning.

Chapter 1

As I drove home, small town water towers and grain elevators dotted the horizon, and treeless cemeteries laid next to recently picked cornfields. The first snow of the season blanketed fields and headstones. Hawks sat on road signs surveying the ditches for dinner, while small dark animals scurried to find hiding places (or so I imagined). Transmission lines along Highway 163 guided my way from Des Moines to Holland, and on to Oskaloosa, where a farmer plowing his field just last summer discovered a mammoth tusk four feet long. Since then, researchers and scientists unearthed more bones at the site. For now, the digging had stopped. It was time to rest. I imagined the trees and plants putting down new roots and sleeping in the silence of the winter season, my favorite season. Spring will come in plenty of time for new growth.

I slowed down, turning off Hwy. 163 onto exit 40, and wound my way home to Holland, Iowa, where I've lived for thirty years. I've been divorced for twenty-five of them and have an ex-husband living in California. Holland is a town of about

18,000 people tucked into a rural community of proud farmers—proud of their farmsteads and the painted white fences that corral their horses, goats, black-faced sheep, and cattle. Unfortunately, the recent recession hit the area hard and all along the highway I saw many fences in need of mending, and many outbuildings in need of fresh paint. Because agriculture is Iowa's number one source of income, we weathered the recession better than most, and things seemed to be on the upswing. Book sales were even on the rise at my book shop. I shouldn't say "my" book shop. Killian Nolan was still the owner.

Killian hired me to work in his book store several years ago. He was a good employer, but he had his dark moods. Eventually, I learned that he and his daughter moved to Iowa directly from Ireland. When she was a teenager, she was raped by a young farmer. The girl ended up committing suicide and Killian wanted revenge. When Killian finally found Doug Garrison, her rapist, alone at the Neal Smith Wildlife Refuge, he knew he couldn't take a man's life. They fought, however, and Killian left Garrison there unconscious. It was Garrison's wife who showed up later and finished off her husband, ending years of domestic abuse. Nevertheless, Killian was now in prison serving a fifty-year term for second-degree murder and must serve seventy percent of the sentence before he's eligible for parole. The merry widow is in for life.

A blast of frigid air hit my face as I got out of my car and skated slowly on the icy driveway to the side door of my house. The days had gotten shorter and at five o'clock, the sky had turned deep blue. It was December twenty-first, winter solstice, after all. I called to Archie, my seven-year-old Golden retriever, as soon as I opened the door, and he ran past me and out the door without so much as a hello. Winter solstice means new beginning to some folks, but just because the earth is tilting as it moves around the sun, and I live in the northern hemisphere that is now getting less sunlight and less warmth, I had a hard time thinking of this day as a new beginning. I'd been Christmas shopping in Des Moines most of the afternoon and was feeling my age. Sixty, in case you're wondering. I threw my purse inside and turned around to get the shopping bags out of the car. Archie came back and sniffed each bag as I navigated the icy stepping stones.

"Good dog, Archie. Did you miss me? Are you hungry? I bet you are." He followed me into the kitchen and lay down by his bowl.

A few flurries whirled in the air as I brought the last of the shopping bags inside and went back out to pull my car into the garage. I wondered when the snow would start falling in earnest. Two weeks ago, the weather gurus doubted we'd have a white Christmas, but suddenly a storm front gathering steam over the Rockies was headed our way, and twelve to sixteen inches of snow were forecast. Christmas was only four days away, so we were almost guaranteed a white Christmas after all. I rejoiced. Both Archie and I love snow.

The ring of the kitchen phone startled me. It was Bobby Hanley, Jasper County's sheriff, letting me know I wouldn't be seeing him that evening because of several car accidents on county roads, and a report of stolen horses from the Johnson farm. I was a little disappointed, but also relieved that I'd have some extra time for Christmas food prep. I had a ton of baking to do, too–cookies, two kinds of fudge and Bobby's favorite pizzelles, the light crispy anise-flavored cookie his Italian grandmother used to make.

"Are you telling me there are people who steal horses in Iowa? We have horse rustlers?" I asked.

He laughed. "It looks that way, Mary Jo. Eight horses are missing from the Johnson farm. Now ask me about the weird part."

"Okay. What's the weird part?"

"An old nag that doesn't belong to the Johnsons was left in the barn."

"Did they think that was a fair exchange?" I joked.

"Well, we'll check it out. We want to get out there to look for tracks before the snow covers them up. The weather is going to get bad tonight, Red. I wish I could see you, but I doubt I'll be finished before midnight." I thought of the first time Bobby nicknamed me Red. It wasn't because my hair is red, although it is, but because I played the role of Red Ryder in a school play many years ago. I hated playing the part of a man in a school play, but I loved that Bobby remembered it.

Most nights, Bobby and I slept separately in our own homes, because he lived in Jasper County, and I lived in Marion County. As sheriff of Jasper County, Bobby was often on call. It was a thirty-minute drive from his front door to mine, and in this weather it would take twice as long. I liked it when Bobby slept over, but I also liked having a whole evening to myself and no one to share the bathroom with.

"It's okay. Just take care of yourself. I have plenty to do to keep me busy. Call me in the morning and don't forget I'm making lasagna for Pippi and Al tomorrow night. You've got it on your schedule, right? Is Al working tonight too?"

"He's going out with me to Johnson's right now. We should be fine for tomorrow night though. I'll call you tomorrow. Love you."

"I love you, too. Be careful, Bobby."

"Will do."

My relationship with Bobby had grown since last May when I unavoidably got entangled in a murder investigation. I just happened to be the person who found a body part of a man on the Neal Smith Wildlife Refuge. I volunteer there in my spare time. Bobby and I still bicker about the "unavoidable" part, but I never *planned* on being part of it. Nor did I plan on getting injured and nearly killed by a woman who had murdered her husband. I should mention that I am an avid mystery reader, and I envision myself as someone with a knack for solving crimes, much to Bobby's dismay. I guess you could say Bobby and I are now an "item," but we've never talked about marriage. We're both content with our independent lives, and although we don't live together, we see each other almost every day, or at least talk on the phone. I turned sixty in May, and I have three grown daughters, Ann, Cara and Pippi, short for Penelope. I decided to phone Pippi, my youngest, later to make sure she knew Al—her boyfriend and Bobby's county deputy—was going to be working late, too. First, I got out my baking ingredients and went to work.

I woke early when Archie jumped onto the bed. He snuggled up against my back—not his usual style. I realized then my nose was ice cold as I glanced at the alarm clock that was as dark as the bedroom. *No electricity? Aargh.*

I found the flashlight in my bedside table drawer, and its beam caught the indoor-outdoor thermometer on my dresser that showed a frigid twenty-two degrees outside and a nippy sixty-two inside. How could I make a lasagna dinner with no electricity, I wondered. Then, it hit me. The roads are probably closed or too icy to drive on anyway. I fished around for my wristwatch on the bathroom counter and saw that it was just a little after seven o'clock.

Snow had fallen all night, and the sky in the east was turning a faint violet blue. Every house, every shrub and every tree was laden with the white stuff. Noni's three-story-high pine bent over like a stooped old man. I was afraid it would break in two when the strong winds blew it from side to side. Noni and Joe Donovan were my elderly next-door neighbors and Noni was my best friend. I could only imagine what the roads must look like. Blowing snow swirled around the house and covered the front porch. Maybe now none of the kids would be able to get here for Christmas.

I'd planned to make lasagna for dinner tonight, the night before Christmas Eve. The girls all loved it, and it had become somewhat of a tradition. However, with the snowstorm, I wasn't sure if everyone would arrive today, or if they should even try to get here. Pippi lived in Des Moines and didn't mind driving in winter conditions with her Toyota 4-Runner. Deputy Al would make it because he loved my daughter, and he loved my lasagna and he didn't live far from me. Bobby would come, but would the kids from Omaha be able to drive through this stuff, and would Ann and Ethan get out of Chicago? I had my doubts.

"Not sure the kids will be coming today, Arch."

He jumped out of bed and barked.

"Sorry, Arch. We'll have to wait and see. We can wrap presents though and go for a walk." I tried to sound enthusiastic, but I wondered when we'd get our electricity back and how cold the house would get in the meantime.

I found heavy socks in a drawer and threw on my warmest bathrobe. Then, I wrapped a shawl around my shoulders and led Archie out to the back porch, so he could do his duty in the fenced-in back yard. I had a hard time getting the storm door open. The snow had piled up against it and literally froze it shut. *Lovely.*

"Come on, Arch. Let's try the side door." *Success.* "You're a good dog for holding it, Archie. Do not go out in the street!" I added emphatically as I pulled the door shut. I didn't want to stand in the open doorway and freeze to death watching my dog relieve himself.

By the time I got a fire going in the wood-burning fireplace, I heard Joe scraping off his driveway with his pickup truck and attached blade. I knew he'd do my drive, too, because we had a deal. Every time he cleared my driveway of snow, I'd make a pot of chili or chowder for him and Noni. I felt I got the better end of the bargain, but I wasn't cooking anything today until my electricity came back on.

I was enjoying the warmth from the fire when my cell phone rang.

Chapter 2

Confident that the caller was Bobby, it took me a second to identify the young male voice.

"Mrs. McGee? I'm snowed in out here and won't be able to open up the Nook this morning. Our road hasn't been plowed yet. I'm sorry—I don't know what to do. Even if I, like, borrowed Al's Jeep, I'm not sure the four-wheel drive could get through these drifts. You should see them."

"Kevin. Hi." I greeted him cheerfully—my first encounter with a human since I woke. I'd hired Kevin last summer after his schizophrenic stepmother had been put in prison for killing his father. "It's okay. Don't worry about it. I doubt if any of the other shops will open today." Kevin Garrison was the most conscientious employee I'd seen, and at eighteen he was the best bookstore salesman I'd hired. Truthfully, he was the *only* book store salesman I'd hired. A freshman at Central College in town, he played basketball for Central's Flying Dutch, number one in Division III football and basketball. During the school's Christmas break, he'd been working almost full-time at the Book Nook giving me much needed time off to prepare for the holidays. He also was the son of Dave Garrison, the man murdered last spring by his second wife who was Kevin's stepmom. Although eighteen years old, Kevin was ill-equipped to live on his own, so when my favorite deputy, bachelor Al Lawson, offered to let Kevin live with him, I was relieved.

"They say we got twelve to fourteen inches last night, but the drifts in our driveway are like three feet high."

"Kevin, don't even try to get out. Do you have electricity?"

"Sure. Don't you?"

"Nope. It went out sometime in the night, but I've got a fire going and Archie and I are keeping warm. I hope it comes back on soon though. No computer, no TV, no stove. Kev, everything I want to do requires electricity."

He laughed. "So, do you think the lights are off all over Holland?"

I had wondered that myself, but there was no way to know. I kicked myself for not having a battery radio in the house.

"I don't know, but I'll call someone to find out. I should get off the phone, Kev, so I don't run my cell down."

"Sure, sure, but what about Stella? If there's no heat in the Nook, she could be getting cold." Of course, I thought. Kevin must care about that cat more than I do. I hadn't even thought of her. She was a stray orange tabby that had free rein of the Book Nook and the apartment above, where Killian used to live.

"Kevin, I'm only about a mile away. If I find out there's no heat uptown, I'll get my skis on and trek up there to check on her. Archie will love a run in the snow anyway." I made Kevin promise not to worry and not to try to get out of Al's driveway until the plows cleared the road. I certainly wouldn't mind a little cross country skiing on the beautiful new snow, but not until the wind died down a bit and the dervish flakes decided to sit one out.

I agreed to call him later to let him know about Stella, and he told me he'd definitely open the Nook the following day. Four days prior to Christmas and people were still shopping for books for gift-giving; and we both agreed that a "snow day" with no sales was not good timing. Christmas wasn't make-or-break time for the book store, but it was close.

I looked out the frosted windows searching for Archie about the same time I heard him barking at the side door.

"Come in here, Archie."

He raced through the door and shook himself free of snow that had gathered on his head and back. I got an old towel from the kitchen and dried him off as best I could while asking him if he found any burrowing voles—his favorite winter pastime. I could tell from the wet and heavy snow on Archie's back shoveling the sidewalk would be difficult—a task I was dreading. With the wind blowing the snow, I couldn't tell if the snow had even stopped falling. I watched as Archie plopped down on the rug and started chewing little balls of ice out from between his claws.

I thought about Stella and knew she could keep warm snuggled up in Killian's old bed clothes, but I wondered if I'd left plenty of food out for her yesterday. *Did I fill her bowl with water*? I couldn't remember. Knowing Kevin was going to open up this morning, I might not have. I stared at the containers of unfrosted sugar cookies on the countertop. I almost heard the muffled santas and angels shouting, "Frost me! Frost me!"

"Sorry, Santa. No electricity. No electric mixer. Maybe later." *Darn. How do the Amish survive?"*

A trip to the basement proved it was too dark down there to wrap the presents I'd stacked on the ping pong table, and I didn't think it made sense to haul them and the wrapping paper upstairs. I was optimistic the lights would come back on soon. I headed back upstairs just in time to hear the back door open and someone stamp their feet on the rug.

"Bobby!" I yelled as I raced up the steps. But it wasn't Bobby standing in my kitchen pulling his parka hood back off his head.

"Just me, Mary Jo. Cold enough for you?" Joe stood at attention on the little braided rug afraid to drip wet snow on the floor.

"Joe. Hi." I took a deep breath, realizing then how much I had wanted to see Bobby. I hoped I didn't seem disappointed to see my neighbor. Joe and Noni lived next door to me from the day my now ex-husband and I moved in twenty-five years ago. At eighty-four, Noni had more get-up and go than women half her age. Her white Dutch boy haircut made her look old-fashioned in a good way.

Joe was short and stout and had lost an arm in a farm accident years ago. Now, he'd removed his old-fashioned, horn-rimmed glasses with his left hand and was fumbling in his coat pocket with his artificial arm for something. I guessed a hanky for wiping his glasses free of snow, and I grabbed a clean dish towel out of a drawer.

"Here, let me do that." I held out my hand for his glasses.

"Thanks, Mary Jo. Just wanted to make sure you're okay with me plowing out your drive now. Noni thinks it's too early because of the wind, but I'd rather do it a second time than wait for it to pile up. She thinks you'd prefer a professional instead of me doing it." He drawled out "professional" and winked at me. I laughed.

"Nope. Not at all. I love the way you do it, Joe, and I wouldn't hire anyone else unless you didn't want to do it anymore. Tell Noni I said so. No, I'll tell her myself when I see her. What's she doing this morning?"

"Just tryin' to keep warm. Sittin' as close to the fireplace as she can without burnin' her knitting. How are you and Killer doin'?" he asked, using his pet name for Archie.

I laughed and we chatted for another minute or two. I assured him we were fine and that I'd be making a pot of clam chowder for him as soon as the electricity came back on. He said that sounded so much better than cold hard cash, as I coaxed him out the door before he got too warm standing inside in his heavy parka and insulated Carhartt overalls.

As I watched Joe climb back into his truck, I wondered what might have kept Bobby from phoning. He said he'd call first thing in the morning, and it was now ten-thirty by my wrist-watch. According to Kevin, Al wasn't home either so I guessed the traffic accidents of the night before had kept them working all night. Then, there was the case of the stolen horses, too. "What's that all about," I said aloud.

Frustrated with not being able to start any Christmas project, I made a snap decision.

"Okay, Arch. We're going skiing to the Book Nook. It'll take me forever to find my boots and long underwear so be patient." He ignored me and persisted in cleaning his paws.

By the time I clicked my boots into the narrow skis on the front lawn, the wind had died down. I stuffed my mittened hands through the pole loops and pushed myself off. This was not only the first time this season for skiing, it was the first time I'd thought about what skiing might feel like on my recently broken ankle. My doctor had given me the go-ahead for any activity, but I still felt a twinge in my ankle whenever I tried anything moderately athletic. Thinking about how I'd broken it six months earlier while trying to escape from that maniacal woman who'd killed her husband gave me shivers—or, maybe it was the twenty-three degree weather. I'd soon find out as Archie and I half walked and half glided up the middle of the street. I breathed in the cold air. It was rough going cutting a trail in the deep snow.

The new snow had muffled the normal outdoor sounds, and all was still as the prairie. I smelled the smoke from wood fireplaces as we passed my neighbors' houses. Wreaths hung from front doors, and unlit Christmas trees stood in many front windows. Not sure when the plows and sanders would be out, I wanted to get going before they ruined this winter wonderland.

I'd brought Archie's leash along, but for now, I was not going to use it. He was happy to stay with me. We passed people shoveling their walks and soon heard snow blowers starting up. By the time we got to the town square, we were both out of breath. We slowed as we passed Vander Heiden's restaurant and the Van Den Berg Gift Shop. We crossed the street that had been plowed earlier but still had plenty of snow for my skis. We glided past Vande Lune Fabrics and Ver Ploeg's Bakery. I swore I could smell cinnamon and sugar cookies.

I loved our town square with its thirty-foot Christmas tree still lit from last night, which was now drooping under mounds of wet snow. Bing Crosby singing, "Where the tree tops glisten and children listen to hear sleigh bells in the snow," came to mind and I started to hum. The square was surrounded by historic shops and bakeries and businesses that dated to the 1800s. Several buildings had typical Dutch facades with festive window displays of greenery, gingerbread houses, and Christmas gifts.

When we reached the Book Nook, we both were winded, but the snow-covered street and shops were so lovely, I took a moment to take it all in and admire my own effort at Christmas window-decorating. I had put every Christmas-and winter-related book in the display, with children's books propped up against small fake Christmas trees. *Olive, the Other Reindeer* and Truman Capote's *A Christmas Memory* shared space with Robert Frost's beautifully illustrated *Stopping by Woods on a Snowy Evening.* The part of the window I loved the most was Bobby's treasured childhood train set he had lent me to set in front of *The Polar Express.* It meant a lot to me when he offered it because his childhood wasn't the greatest. That train set was one of very few gifts from his parents. Seeing it in the window made me think about Bobby and wonder what he was doing.

I clicked out of my skis and wiped them down with my mitten before unlocking the door with its cheerful wreath. Archie pushed his way in ahead of me and waited for a word about our agenda. I switched on the light just inside the door, and laughed when I remembered there was no power. I pulled my fleece hat off and shook snow onto the large black mat. I unzipped my jacket pocket, fished my cell phone out and punched in Bobby's number while I headed toward the cash register.

"Hey, Mary Jo. I was just thinking of calling you." Bobby sounded tired or frustrated or both and from the background noise, I could tell he was in his car. If I was upset he hadn't phoned me, I quickly forgave him realizing the circumstances of his job.

"You sound tired, Bobby. Are you driving?" I felt something touch my ankle and I jumped. It was just Stella. She meowed so I picked her up and headed for the stuffed chair in the children's section.

"Yep. I'm headed out to the Johnson place to check on those missing horses. That eighteen-car pileup on eighty last night kept us busy all night. The whole crew was out working it. Why is it accidents, shoplifting, drug dealing always increase around the holidays?'

"And horse rustling? Does that increase around the holidays, too?"

"Hey, hey. Good one, Red. I have no idea as this is the first horse rustling case I've ever been involved in. But, as soon as I talk to Johnson and file a report, I'm headed back to my place to catch a few hours sleep. Any sign of lights coming back on in Holland yet?"

"Not that I can see," I said as I looked out the front window onto the street. I could hear a noisy snowplow in the distance. "Stop that," I whispered as Stella started licking my face.

"Well, if you're still without heat tonight, you and Archie can spend the night with me. Sound okay?"

"Sure, but I'm still hoping the lights will come on and we can still have our lasagna dinner with Pippi and Al. I'm also hoping Cara and Ted and Ann and Ethan will make it, too."

"Have you heard from Pippi? Because even if your lights come back on, Pippi should not drive down. Des Moines didn't get hit as bad as we did, but the highways are all in pretty bad shape. One sixty-three is eighty-percent ice and snow packed.

I'm sorry to give you the bad news, Mary Jo, but no one should be on the roads today."

I pulled in a deep breath. He's right. *What was I thinking*?

"It's okay. Not your fault the gods are against me. I'll call Pippi right now. Tell Al we'll try again tomorrow night."

"I sent him home, Red. He was a walking zombie, and, I'm almost at that point, too."

"You're not going out to Johnsons alone, are you?"

"Sure I am. Why wouldn't I? It's a case of missing horses. We don't need the FBI."

He laughed. I hesitated. I hated sounding like a nervous Nellie, but when DCI Agent Frances Curoe went to a farm to investigate a murder this past summer, she ended up being killed. Possibly reading my mind, Bobby interrupted my thoughts. "It's a case of stolen horses, Red. Not murder. I plan to be back home and asleep in bed in two hours tops. Trust me, Red, I was in more danger last night sliding around on icy roads and dodging cars and trucks speeding to get to grandma's house for Christmas than I will be today filing a report of missing horses."

"Hmm. Okay. There were no fatalities last night, were there?"

"No, sweetie, just minor injuries. Gotta go, Mary Jo. I love you. I'll call you late this afternoon after I get some sleep."

I was admiring the Christmas tree in the corner that Kevin and Noni had helped me decorate. It smelled faintly of balsam pine and I checked its stand for water. Wishing there was electricity so I could turn on its lights, I jumped when a loud noise erupted. Archie barked and looked up at me. The radio. Killian's old radio must have been on when the electricity went off. I flicked on the overhead lights and heard the furnace come to life. I walked over to the table to turn down the volume of the Christmas music when I heard the words *weather update*.

KPNO's weather update! A cold front and low pressure system continues to move in from the Rockies. Snow will continue to fall off and on throughout the day, with temperatures dropping into the single digits by evening. Accumulations from ten to sixteen inches are predicted for central Iowa with more to the east. At present, Interstate 80 is one hundred percent snow and ice packed. The highway patrol recommends staying off it although it is still open.

"Well, that doesn't sound good, does it, Arch?" He wagged his tail.

"Right. You love snow. I forgot." Stella had fallen asleep on my lap and barely moved when I raised myself gently out from under her. I filled her water bowl and added kibble to her food dish. The shop would soon be warm, and Kevin would come to get her when he could.

"Let's head home and get those cookies frosted. Even if no one else makes it to dinner, Joe and Noni will come. Unless their sidewalk gets too icy for them to navigate." *Why was I talking to Archie like he understood*? Sometimes I thought he could. I knew he sensed my feelings, and right now he knew we were heading back home.

Chapter 3

Sheriff Bob Hanley drove his black Pathfinder carefully over the newly plowed road. The snow had fallen after the ice storm so the plows were having trouble getting through the thick layer of ice underneath the snow, making the road good in certain places and an obstacle course in other spots. It was like driving down a railroad track. The struts took the brunt of it, and, being in no hurry, he took it slow. Tired, but not too tired to remember who Harvey Johnson was, he mentally reviewed what facts he already knew. Johnson had gone missing last June without a trace. No ransom note even though Johnson was a millionaire. He was president and CEO of a huge tractor parts company in Newtown. In recent years, he'd spent money unwisely putting the company at risk of going under, but the company had recently expanded and was flourishing, according to the latest reports. Harvey Johnson was sixty-two years old, divorced with three children, and owned several horses evidently. Whether this was a hobby or for income, Bobby would have to find out. After an extensive search, no trace of Harvey Johnson dead or alive had turned up. It was Johnson's son, Harvey Junior, who reported the missing horses.

Hanley kept the connection between Harvey Johnson and Johnson's missing horses from Mary Jo. Common enough name. There was no need to worry her. She'd been pretty jumpy since finding part of a body on the local refuge's prairie last May. Not to mention getting herself nearly killed by the murderer in a barn. He didn't want her to think there was a killer at the Johnsons' waiting for him to show up, although many people suspected a family member of killing Harvey in order to "up" their status in the heir department. However, no one could prove that theory and all three adult children were cleared of wrongdoing. That left Harvey Johnson's ex-wife, whose only motive could have been overdue alimony payments, but killing off the source didn't seem the best way to get alimony flowing again. No, Sheriff Hanley was pretty sure no family member was involved in Johnson's disappearance, but without a body, not much could be proved one way or the other. The question in his mind now: Were the missing horses connected to Harvey Senior's disappearance?

He spotted the farm from a distance. Two red brick ranch-style houses popular in the sixties sat side by side off the highway. Unassuming, they didn't look like millionaires' homes, but one was the home of Harvey Johnson, Sr., and the other belonged to Harvey Junior. Hanley pulled off the main road onto a frontage road, drove several more yards and turned into the plowed driveway between the two houses. As he got closer to the houses, the paved drive changed to a bricked herringbone pattern. *Must be heated too as there was no snow on it.* Nice, he thought. The driveway curved to the attached garage on the side of the larger home and, as he pulled to a stop, he realized it was at least a five-car garage. It must have been added on recently. It was not visible from the highway. He guessed the house also had a new addition behind the garage. As he stepped out of the Pathfinder to take a closer look, he heard someone behind him shout above the wind. He grabbed his department-issued brown watch cap and pulled it down over his ears. No way would the brisk wind let him wear his broad-brimmed Smokey Bear hat.

"Are you here about my horses?"

Hanley turned and saw who must be Harvey Junior stepping out the side door of the smaller house pulling on a red puffy jacket. Hanley headed toward him.

"Sheriff Hanley," Bobby said holding out his hand. "You must be Harvey Johnson Junior?" They shook hands as Hanley studied his face. Hanley had seen photos of Harvey Johnson Senior in the newspapers over the years—ribbon cuttings, fund-raisers and such. Harvey Junior was the spitting image of his father with dark brown hair cut short, a receding hairline, heavy black eyebrows, blue eyes and a large chin that jutted outward. Hanley put him in the six foot range noticing that his rubber boots were thick soled and possibly added an inch. Junior pulled a tan seed corn cap out of his coat pocket and put it on.

"Call me Junior. Everyone does. Even my wife." He smiled. "I thought you'd be here last night, but figured with the snow storm, you might have your hands full. I'd like to find those horses before someone gets them to Canada or Mexico, you know."

"Why would someone take them to Canada or Mexico?" Hanley asked stamping his feet to keep them warm. Johnson must have noticed and quickly invited the sheriff to step inside. Grateful to be out of the cold, and eager to see what kind of house a millionaire lived in, Hanley followed Johnson inside. He noticed an ancient faded, fake green wreath hanging on the storm door with a shredded red bow flapping in the wind. Two steps inside the side door took them into a long kitchen with a row of cupboards on one side and appliances on the other. The room ended with a small maple table and four chairs. Guess millionaires don't live much different from the rest of us, Hanley thought.

"Have a seat, Sheriff. Coffee?" Johnson asked pointing to a pot on the counter. Hanley would have preferred tea but anything hot sounded good, and he was grateful for the offer.

"Sure. Black is fine." He looked around for signs of Mrs. Johnson but didn't see or hear her. Other than the wreath on the door, which had seen better days, there was no Christmas *décor*, as Mary Jo called it. There was a small wooden gun case mounted on the paneled wall opposite the kitchen table. It held three guns. Hanley knew it wasn't unusual for farmers to have arms, but he would like to have taken a closer look and was concerned that they weren't under lock and key. For now though, he just wanted to find out more about the missing horses.

Johnson took two brown chipped ceramic mugs from a cupboard and poured the coffee. Setting one down in front of the sheriff, he said, "Mexico and Canada so he can sell them for horse meat is what I'm afraid of. He can't sell 'em around here because people would recognize 'em as mine."

Not wanting to ignore the elephant in the room which was Johnson's missing parent, Hanley asked, "Are the horses yours or did they belong to your father?"

"They were my dad's. He loved horses and started buying them for me and my sisters when we were teenagers. Thought horses could keep us out of mischief."

"Did they?"

Johnson chuckled. "To some extent, I guess they did." It's pretty hard to smoke pot or tie one on when you have to rope calves or barrel race the next day." He paused and frowned as if he was thinking of something unpleasant. He looked closely into Sheriff Hanley's eyes. "Have you found any new leads about my dad? The last time I checked, I was told there weren't any. I decided not to call anymore until after the holidays. We want to get through them as best we can. My girls deserve that, but if you have any news, I'd like to hear it now." Hanley remembered the Johnsons had twin daughters in college.

"No, I'm sorry. There are no new leads. We thought you'd eventually get a ransom note, but without a note and no leads and no body, we're at a standstill. He almost hated to say what was next. He didn't believe in giving people false hope, but this time, during the holiday season, he wanted to give a young family some reason to believe, and he truly felt some optimism, so he continued, "since we haven't found his body, there is still hope that he's alive."

"Let me stop you there, Sheriff. I personally have given up hope that Dad is alive. Six months now. That's a long time. He would not have run away." Johnson spoke vehemently and ran his fingers through his hair. "He isn't in hiding. There was no crime or embezzlement that he would be running from. If he was kidnapped for ransom, we'd have heard by now. No, my dad is dead. I'd bet money on it." Appearing despondent, he'd run out of steam by the time he ended his thoughts, and slowly shook his head back and forth.

"I understand why you feel that way. I'd give anything to be able to tell you differently, but there's nothing new right now. The few leads we had were all dead end." Hanley paused. "It does seem odd that now you have eight horses missing. Can you think of any connection they might have to your father's disappearance?" Hanley secretly thought this could be the new lead they'd been hoping for in the missing man's case.

Harvey Junior looked up. "None. I've racked my brain. I can't think clearly. It's just so weird, and then to have that old paint left in the shed. Who would do that? And why?"

"Old paint?"

"The old horse that was left. Not familiar with horses, are you, Sheriff?"

Hanley laughed. He was definitely not familiar with horses. Never had them or been around them, but this was as good a time as any to get familiar with them. In the next hour, he learned about colts, mares, stallions, geldings, and ponies. Names he'd heard over the years like sorrel, palomino and roan he now knew were colors of horses, not breeds. Johnson had a way with words and the two men could be seen laughing together by Johnson's wife who stared out the frosted window watching them as they walked toward the barns and corral. Hanley asked questions he knew were stupid, but he was trained to ask questions. To not ask questions is stupid.

"Why do people change a stallion into a gelding?" He'd always wanted to know, but wasn't sure how to word the question. They stood inside the small shed surveying the lonely old paint who watched them out of suspicious eyes.

Johnson actually snorted. "Because stallions are unruly and horny and cause chaos."

"Ah."

"Do you know why quarter horses are called quarter horses?"

Hanley smiled and shook his head.

"The horses in the Wild West were small and could only run for a quarter of a mile. Today, they are cross-bred with thoroughbreds so they're larger and can run further, but still called quarter horses."

"So what kind of horses went missing yesterday and what are they worth?" Hanley pulled a notepad and pencil out of his inside jacket pocket and thumbed it open.

Johnson paused and thought before he answered.

"Eight horses total. Three were three-year-old roan Appaloosas worth, oh, roughly a thousand each. Three were quarter horses trained for roping steers and catching calves and were worth maybe $10,000 to $15,000 each. And two were thoroughbreds that Dad bought just last June before he disappeared. He really admired them. They were worth the most, and because they're trained to race, they might be worth more to the right buyer."

Hanley scribbled his notes quickly, his bare fingers feeling the sting of the Arctic air. "Did you see any tracks in the snow last night?"

"No. Snow was really falling heavy though. Any tracks would've filled in by the time I noticed the horses were missing. I check every night after supper. It was dark last night, but I looked for tracks. Didn't see any."

"How would someone remove eight horses from here?"

"Two four-horse trailers would do it, or one bigger trailer could fit all eight."

Not seeing any sign of foul play or any blood in the barn or surrounding area, Hanley had an idea.

"How do farmers get rid of dead horses?"

"Hell, they just dig a hole with a backhoe and bury them, or they call a rendering truck to come get 'em. There's a guy up in northwest Iowa who hauls four semis of healthy horses that nobody wants up to Canada each week to sell for meat. Forty to a semi."

"Why would someone send a healthy horse up to Canada?"

"Don't want it no more or can't afford to feed it. You tell me." He said disgustedly. "Plus, it's profitable for horse traders."

In the next ten minutes, Sheriff Hanley discovered that it doesn't cost a lot to feed a horse in the winter—even with two feet of snow on the ground, they eat mostly hay and grain once a day. Hanley noticed the old paint had a good supply of hay in her steel pen. The horse appeared to be sleeping, so he just had to ask.

"Is it true horses sleep standing up?"

"Yeah, they do. They lock their joints, but they also can lay down to sleep, too. Sheriff, if you don't have any other questions, I promised Jean I'd drive her to the store for a few things. She's not much for driving in these conditions, you know?"

"Harvey," Hanley began, "I mean Junior. Could I talk to your wife? Jean? I have a few questions for her, it'll only take a minute or two."

Harvey Junior took a deep breath and crossed his arms. Hanley recognized a defensive stance when he saw one and waited to see what response Junior came up with.

"Sorry, Sherriff. She hasn't been herself lately, and I don't want to upset her this close to Christmas. Could it wait 'til after the holidays? She doesn't know anything about the horses. I don't think she could be of much help."

"Sure. Sure. It can wait. Just one more question. Can you think of anyone who would steal your horses? Anybody have a grudge against you? Anything you can think of that might help us find them?"

They walked slowly toward Hanley's Pathfinder. It had started snowing again, but lightly now, and flakes collected on the men's hats and shoulders.

"No. I was asked the same question when Dad disappeared. I can't think of anyone. The neighbors all are friendly, and I've known them my whole life."

"Well, we'll start by talking to each of your neighbors within a three or four-mile radius to see if anyone knows or has heard anything. Call me if you think of anything that might help." Hanley scribbled his phone number on his pad and tore the sheet off and handed it to Johnson, anxious to pull his glove back on. "How's your mother, by the way?"

"Mom? She's fine, I guess. She's on a Christmas cruise in the Caribbean."

Hanley got the message that Junior didn't want to discuss his mother, or maybe he was just in a hurry. Hanley remembered Mrs. Johnson Sr. as being a person who thought of herself as a victim when her husband went missing six months ago. She was short and slightly overweight. In her late fifties or early sixties, her hair was thick and black as coal. It was shoulder length, and she seemed to purposely swing her head around to illustrate how beautiful her hair was. He guessed it was a wig. He also remembered the gold bracelets that lined her forearms and the rings on all her fingers. Last June, she'd been more tan than most folks in the area—maybe after spending the winter in Arizona was his guess. Maybe she even had a facelift or two. He hadn't liked interviewing her then and didn't see any reason why he'd need to interview her again about the horses.

On his way back to town, Hanley made a mental note to get Al and any other available deputy to canvas the neighboring farmers. Someone had to know something. He'd often thought such was the case after a crime had been committed, and most of the time, it was true. He also needed to find out what those horses were insured for. He liked Harvey Junior, but he couldn't rule him out as a suspect, and he was clearly protecting his wife. Why?

The wind had died down. Snow was falling again, softly and quietly. I stood at the kitchen window and breathed in the beauty of it. Everything was white and sparkly in the sun. Joe and Noni's house looked like a picture book gingerbread house complete with white icing sloping gently off the roof. Archie napped in his favorite spot in front of the kitchen fireplace. I loved this house, this town, and the people in it.

The telephone jarred me out of my daydreaming, and I was happy to hear Bobby's voice.

"Hi, Red! Are you frosting cookies yet?" He sounded out of breath.

"No, I thought I'd let you try your hand at it this year," I teased.

"Ha. I'd love that if I had the time, but," he paused, "things are getting more complicated, and I need to talk to you about one of the complications. It's a good complication in my view. I hope you agree."

My stomach seemed to clench up as I waited for him to continue. I'm no different from most women I know—we want the holidays to be perfect like our memories of childhood Christmases. They were never really perfect, but children don't notice the imperfections—the overdone turkey or the pile of prematurely dead needles under the Christmas tree. I didn't have a good feeling about a *good* complication three days before Christmas. Wasn't a *good complication* an oxymoron like bittersweet? "I'll just spit it out. Scottie is coming home for Christmas, Mary Jo."

My mouth opened but nothing came out except, "Whoo?" I sounded like an owl. Oh, I knew who Bobby meant, but I was surprised to say the least. Scott was his thirty-four-year-old son who lived in Las Vegas. He worked, last I'd heard, as a security guard for one of the big casinos. He'd been married briefly and divorced. No children. As a teenager, he'd been in trouble more often than the average small town teenager. Scott's problems revolved around drinking too much, smoking too much pot, driving too fast and skipping too many classes. Bobby and Sharon always bailed him out, but then Sharon was killed in a car accident and Bobby seemed to have given up on Scott; eventually, he kicked Scott out of their house when he was twenty and had flunked out of Iowa State. I couldn't remember the last time Scott came home for a visit, or the last time Bobby mentioned talking with him.

"Scott? Coming home for Christmas? When?"

Bobby laughed. "He gets in tonight about five. I thought I could bring them over for your lasagna dinner." I could hear the happiness in Bobby's voice. His jolly good mood was contagious and I giggled. "Of course, that could change if their flight gets cancelled, but it sounds like the weather is clearing up and flights are back on time. I just checked online. Like I said, that could change." He paused while waiting for my reaction. "Mary Jo?"

"I'm here, Bobby. But, who's coming with him? You said *them*. You'd bring *them* over to dinner."

"Oh. Sorry. I forgot. I'm kind of rushed here right now, Red. Scottie has a girlfriend. He's bringing his girlfriend. I gotta run now, but I'll call you later. It's all right, isn't it? If Scott and his friend come to dinner? You usually have plenty, right?" He laughed a little nervously.

I assured him there would be plenty of food and that it was great Scott was coming. I felt my heart flutter and my stomach did something similar. *Butterflies? Nah, curious maybe, but not nervous.*

"What's his girlfriend's name?" I asked hurriedly.

"Tennille."

"Tennille? Like in The *Captain and Tennille*?"

"I guess. I hadn't thought of that. Look, I really have to run."

We hung up with Bobby's promise to call me later. He'd sounded so happy, and why wouldn't he be? If any of my three girls had been absent from my life for as many years as Scott had been from Bobby's life, I'd be thrilled she was coming home for Christmas. So, why was I feeling resentful? Was I worried Scott would cause a problem? That was not a far-fetched worry. He'd always seemed to be surrounded by bad influences and problems his whole life.

Glancing at the clock, I realized I'd better get those cookies frosted and start the lasagna, but before I could get out the mixer, Ann phoned with the news I'd been expecting. Their flight was cancelled out of O'Hare. She and Ethan would not be flying out until possibly Christmas day, but she'd keep me posted. As soon as we hung up, the phone rang again. This time it was Cara to say they had made it to Des Moines with no trouble, and would arrive in Holland as soon as possible. They were going to get a bite to eat and hit the road again. I told her what Bobby had said about the roads, and she promised they'd be careful. I silently prayed they wouldn't have an accident, and I started the tedious job of frosting Christmas cutout cookies.

I divided my white frosting into two small bowls. Into one, I added a few drops of green food color, and into the other I added a few drops of red, which made the white icing look pink, of course. By the time I'd frosted and decorated five dozen cookies, my back ached so I stretched out on the sofa and rested before putting water on to boil for the lasagna noodles.

When the lasagna was ready to go into the oven, I remembered Martha Stewart's advice for dinner parties: set the table first. Even if dinner is delayed, guests will see the table is ready and feel relieved. Well, that is what Martha said. Lord knows, I don't want my family feeling worried that dinner is delayed. Besides, setting the table is my favorite part of dinner parties. As I placed the white dinner plates on the green and red quilt I used as a tablecloth, I worried we wouldn't all fit at one table. There would be Pippi and Al, Bobby and me, Cara and Ted, and the two little boys Max and Noah, Joe and Noni, and now Scott and Tennille. Twelve people. My kitchen table could extend that long, but it would be crowded. I could serve the lasagna from the stove, and pass the salad to save space. A wooden bowl of baguettes and focaccia would fit on the table. Now the red goblets that have been in my family for three generations. Silverware. Voila! Martha would be proud.

Time flew and, in what seemed like minutes instead of hours, the kitchen door flew open with Max and Noah rushing in ahead of their parents. Archie started barking and ran with his tail awaggin' to the boys. There was much commotion as we took care of coats and suitcases and gift-wrapped packages. I breathed a sigh of relief that they had arrived safely, and we all celebrated with cookies and milk.

Al and Pippi, looking very much in love, were the next to arrive with Kevin, who immediately let Archie outside to play in the snow with him. Al was dressed casually in khakis and a red plaid long-sleeved shirt with a red quilted vest looking very Christmasy, and Pippi looked her usual beautiful self. Pippi was tall and thin and fair-skinned like me, but that is where the resemblance ended. Her style could only be called *Bohemian*, and tonight she was attired in black leggings under a short blue and white silk wrap-around kimono. Her long reddish hair was braided and wound round her head like a German *hausfrau*. A few strands of hair came loose and framed her face. Her red sparkly earrings looked like a stripper's tassels. She looked absolutely stunning. She'd always hated her fair freckly complexion, but seemed to have accepted her genetic makeup with age. I took their coats back to my bedroom while they pulled off their boots and lined them up beside the others. Then, we all got busy.

Al happily brought extra chairs up from the basement while Pippi put on some Christmas music. She helped with the salad while we waited for the others. Kevin had let Archie back in and he was happily rolling around on the living room rug with Max and Noah. Archie was trying to lick their faces as Bing Crosby crooned "I'm dreaming of a white Christmas" in the background. Al took on the role of bartender and was heating apple cider on the stove, and he had already told Ted to help himself to a cold beer from an ice cooler on the back porch. A bottle of apple brandy stood next to the cider for anyone wanting something stronger.

"Would you like me to decant this bottle of red we brought, Mrs. Mac?"

I stared at him. "Oh, sure," I said, as soon as I figured out he meant uncork the bottle. Al loves vocabulary and always uses the correct word. He also goes by the book. It's what makes him a good deputy and what makes Bobby appreciate working with him on cases. There is never a misunderstanding when Al is doing the talking. I've come to appreciate that quality in him, too.

Joe and Noni were the next to arrive each carrying an armload of fresh evergreens. "They fell off our trees in the storm so why not make use of them?" Noni asked.

"Oh, they're beautiful, Noni. And they smell so good too. Pippi, could you put some down the center of the table?"

"Sure. I think." She looked dubiously at the already crowded table, but started tucking in small branches here and there.

Noni wore her red plaid skirt and green Christmas sweater with the huge Santa on the front. Her white hair framed her face. She looked beautiful and had a glow about her. Mary Jo realized there was no connection between age and beauty and Noni was the proof. Joe was in his usual bib overalls, but looked festive in a red and green plaid flannel shirt. Plaid and flannel seemed *de rigueur* for the night. I looked down at my Christmas apron covering my jeans and white shirt and decided it would have to do. Joe and Noni's cheeks were rosy from their short walk next door. Cara ran to get her camera, and her first shot was of Joe and Noni toasting each other with mugs of warm cider.

Soon, we had all settled down to wait for Bobby's arrival with Scott and Tennille. I looked at the others and wondered if they all knew how anxious I was about meeting Scott again. No, they all looked oblivious which made me feel better.

I was just checking the lasagna in the oven when Bobby burst through the side door into the kitchen with Scott and a very young woman behind him. They stomped their feet on the rag rug longer than necessary. Maybe they were nervous, too. The young woman wore open-toe high heeled shoes and a tan trench coat. She looked like she was freezing.

And, she looked pregnant.

Chapter 4

Here, let me take your coats," Pippi and Cara both piped. They had never looked alike and had never shared common interests, but they both knew how to fill an awkward spot. Bobby pulled me to him and gave me a cold peck on my cheek. Cold and light like a snowflake, I thought.

"Let me, Pippi." Bobby helped Tennille out of her coat and asked, "Mary Jo, you remember Scott?" Scott held out his hand as if to tell me he was not interested in a hug. "And this is Tennille," Bobby continued with the introductions. "Scott's girlfriend from Las Vegas." We all greeted her warmly, and Pippi gave her a big hug. "This is Mary Jo, Pippi and Cara. That's my deputy, Al Lawson, running the blender." Al waved greetings and went back to his concoctions. "And Cara's husband, Ted," who had just come around the corner into the kitchen with Noah and Max hanging onto his legs. The boys were laughing and screaming something unintelligible.

Scott was as handsome as ever but even though a cowboy hat and Western boots would not normally look out of place in

Iowa, his did. It was a show-offy cowboy hat with a silver and turquoise trimmed band, not a working cowboy hat. Same with the white and black boots. They looked like snakeskin. Well, he does live in Las Vegas, I thought.

With introductions over, Bobby headed back to my bedroom with an armful of coats saying he was going to change out of his uniform. The rest of us moved into the living room to visit with Joe and Noni, sip our drinks and munch on Cara's sweet and salty pecans. The cider tasted of Christmas and snow and houses warmed by burning wood. I thanked Al for bringing it, as I tried not to stare at Tennille. She was very pretty in a sulky way with dark brown hair cut into a short pixie style making her brown eyes appear huge. The purple highlights in her hair matched the tight purple knit dress stretched across her very pregnant tummy. She wasn't much over eighteen, I suspected. A small tattoo peeped out from her V neckline. Her large breasts might have resulted from her advanced pregnancy. Or not.

When Bobby came out of my bedroom, having changed into civilian clothes, Scott looked surprised and announced, "Dad must have a set of clothes in all his girlfriends' houses." No one laughed. Bobby didn't offer any rebuttal, but he stammered and tried to move on by starting a conversation about horses. That seemed to enthrall Max and Noah, but I remained speechless.

"Ah, um, Noah, did you know a horse weighs between 800 and 2,000 pounds? That heavier one would be a Clydesdale draft horse like the kind you see on TV in the beer commercials pulling a wagon." Bobby glanced at me, "and, they have to go to the dentist to have their teeth pulled or fixed."

"Really? How do they get to the dentist?" Max asked.

"Haven't you ever seen a horse trailer being pulled by a pickup truck in Nebraska? That's how." The boys nodded and asked more questions. I learned horses can live to be thirty-five years old, but a hard-working draft horse probably wouldn't live past fifteen. I loved that Bobby was entertaining the boys, but I also knew he was uncomfortable with Scott's comment about his having extra clothes in all his girlfriends' houses and was covering up for it.

Soon, Bobby and Al were discussing the case about the missing horses, talking in quiet voices like they didn't want anyone to hear. Without trying to, I noticed Scott was on his third drink when we all sat down at the kitchen table. Pippi had taken Tennille under her wing and was offering to lend her a pair of boots and a warmer coat while she was visiting our colder climate. Tennille said very little, but she seemed appreciative of Pippi for the offer and for Pippi's friendship. Scott was totally ignoring Tennille which made the rest of us pay more attention to her.

I listened to the ting of the sleet hitting my bedroom window and tried to sleep, but sleep eluded me. Dinner had seemed to drag on. Scott had the habit of saying "Uh-uh-uh-uh" when he was talking. It was irritating and it annoyed me. He also complained about how hard it was to get a beer in Holland. "You have to drive to Knoxville for a beer," he groused. Well, it's true there are no bars in Holland, but there are restaurants where you could get a beer—maybe not on the grand scale of Las Vegas, however. Dutch Reformed are not a drinking crowd, but plenty of people in Holland enjoy their libations.

Tennille told me the lasagna was great. She also said the house was great. The Christmas tree was great. Their flight was great. When they left, she thanked me for the great dinner including the great peppermint brownie dessert. Scott had difficulty pulling on his cowboy boots, and I wondered if I was the only one who noticed. I wasn't sure how much wine Scott drank with dinner, but I secretly hoped Bobby would be doing the driving. As everyone headed out the door exchanging Christmas greetings, Scott turned around and grabbed Pippi in a rough embrace. It was inappropriate and I almost lost my cool, but Pippi handled it by pushing him away and calling for Al to get her coat. She'd already lent her boots to Tennille with a promise to drop a warm coat off for her tomorrow. Before Pippi and Al left, she'd rooted through my closet for a pair of my boots to tide her over.

"I need a new pair anyway, right Mom?" I wasn't sure if she did or didn't but Tennille probably felt better about taking Pippi's warm boots, and it also sounded like a good idea for Pippi's Christmas present. It would have to be a late gift though. I was not going shopping on Christmas Eve even if I, too, could use a new pair of boots.

I looked out the door at the snow which had started falling again.

Now, tree branches, burdened with heavy wet snow broke and fell to the ground with despair. I got out of bed and looked out the window at the steel gray sky. I didn't mind that Bobby wasn't spending the night with me, but I missed him. Of course, he would go back to his house with Scott and Tennille. Cara and Ted and the boys were upstairs sound asleep. Noah and Max were looking forward to the Christmas Eve festivities tomorrow. Ted had answered all their questions about the snowman contest that they intended to participate in and explained that Sinter Klauss might look a little different from the santa they were used to seeing. Archie had chosen to sleep with the boys instead of me, much to the boys' delight. Scott and Tennille mentioned they were flying back to Vegas on Monday, so they were only going to be here for three days. Surely, I couldn't begrudge Bobby three days with his son. I crawled back under the covers to my still-warm spot. It felt good, and I fell asleep quickly.

Chapter 5

Max and Noah watched *The Grinch Who Stole Christmas* on TV in the living room while Ted put some peanut butter and red currant jelly sandwiches together for our lunch. Cara, who liked healthier fare, made her quinoa and fig salad, while I made roasted tomato soup. The kitchen still smelled of last night's lasagna and the log fire, but new aromas permeated the air. I breathed it all in as I listened to the Grinch song from the living room. "You're a rotter, Mr. Grinch," and "You stink, stank, stunk!"

As soon as the movie was over, the boys came running into the kitchen.

"Grandma, what's a rotter?" asked five-year-old Max.

I'd often wondered that myself, and I decided to look it up.

"I don't know. Let's look it up in the dictionary, shall we?" I wiped my hands on the nearest towel.

"Why don't we just google it?" asked Noah. Then they were off begging Cara for the use of her iPad. Well, times are a-changin' I thought to myself. *Will dictionaries become extinct like the do-do bird?*

"A rotter is a cruel unpleasant person, Grandma," said Noah.

"Noah is a rotter. Noah is a rotter," yelled Max.

"Noah is NOT a rotter, Max. He isn't cruel and he isn't unpleasant either. Are you, Noah?" I asked.

"Max is the rotter. He ate all my purple M&Ms from the gold and purple ones you gave me for the Viking's games. He ate every purple one, Grandma!"

"Max, why did you eat all the purple ones?" I asked.

"Because he's a rotter!" Noah answered with a superior attitude as he strutted out of the kitchen with Max on his tail.

I sighed and gazed out the window over the kitchen sink with my little pots of herbs on its ledge. The snow fell lazily on the cars in the driveway. This was going to be a white Christmas for sure, I mused happily.

Sheriff Hanley headed south on Highway 14 out of Newtown toward Monroe to pick up Al. The sun had been shining earlier, and he'd squinted at the bright snow-covered lawn as he pulled out of his driveway. Now, the pelting snow had started again, and his wipers slapped back and forth to keep up. He was glad his SUV had four-wheel drive when he saw the condition of the highway. Wind had blown snow onto the road in drifts three feet high in places. He remembered that the DeGroot farm had a long gravel lane, and he hoped it would be clear.

Scott and Tennille were still asleep in the guest room when he left at eight o'clock. They'd had a long day yesterday flying from Las Vegas, Tennille being pregnant and all. Not to mention the amount of wine and beer Scott consumed at Mary Jo's last night. Bobby worried about his son and his drinking, and he was determined to have a man-to-man with him later that afternoon. He would have preferred to postpone this visit to DeGroots, but investigations don't take a break for holidays.

He pulled into Al's driveway and hit the brakes gently as he skidded to a stop on the ice. Al stepped out his front door before Bobby even had his car in park. Al was pulling on his regulation brown parka as he bounced down his front steps. A brown knit watch cap with the county sheriff's insignia covered his shaved head, and he wore brown waterproof boots. Bobby was grateful for a deputy like Al who was always dressed for the "elements" as Al liked to say. They often needed boots in winter, but today they planned to not only question the DeGroots, but search their barns and outbuildings as well. Boots would be essential. Al gave the snow-covered passenger side window a swipe with his glove and climbed into the car with a shiver.

"Brrr. Winter sure blew in."

"You got that right, but we knew it was coming. How are you and Kevin managing with just one car I mean?" Bobby backed out of the driveway.

"Good. Good. No problems."

"You don't sound convinced." They were back on the highway, and Al buckled his seat belt.

A silence settled on the front seat between them as Bobby slowed for wind-swept drifts and then speeded up to gain lost time.

"Anything you want to talk about, Al?"

Al gazed out at the snow-covered fields and pastures, and thought about telling his boss, his friend, about catching Kevin smoking pot one night and his suspicion that Kevin was skipping classes, but he also thought this wasn't a good time. Bobby had enough on his hands right now. They passed a snowmobiler speeding up and down through the ditch beside the road. It looked like fun. Maybe that would be something he could do with Kevin some time. He was feeling a bit of a failure as far as Kevin was concerned. What did he know about teenage boys after all, other than the fact that he'd once been one himself?

They slowed down behind a plow spitting sand out its spreader.

"It's nothing, Sheriff." Al paused and took a deep breath. "What do we know about these missing horses, so far? I came up with nothing yesterday, but I only interrogated the VanderMeeks so far. They're Johnsons' second closest neighbors. The DeGroots live about a quarter mile away. Bill VanderMeek has only one machine shed now and one small barn for geese. He's been retired for, let's see now." He pulled a small notepad out of his parka's chest pocket. "Retired twenty-seven years ago. Sold all his stock and rents out the land. I can't see him rustling horses or rustling anything. Lives with his wife and, like I said, a gaggle of geese."

Bobby laughed as they pulled onto the shoulder. "Did we pass it? We should be close by now. Johnsons' place is just over there," he said, pointing to the horizon. DeGroots' lane must be here somewhere."

They drove on a few more yards and spotted the lane with a mailbox almost buried in snow that a plow had banked up along the road. It was a long lane, but they could see a house and farm buildings about a quarter mile in the distance. Bobby tightened his grip on the steering wheel as he swerved and skidded, slowing almost to a stop.

"Merry Christmas!" he said dejectedly. He looked over at Al. "What do you think? Can we make it?"

"I'd try. We can always call for backup if we get stuck, although I'd hate calling Jamie on Christmas Eve. What do you think?"

"I think we'll give it a try. Hang on."

The lane was drifted heavily in places but not so bad in others. It wound through several rolling fields of corn and pasture and turned at a right angle toward the farm. A few tense minutes later, they breathed easier as they pulled up to a small mint green ranch house with smoke rising from its chimney. There were no cars in sight. Two white sheets and two pillowcases hung frozen on the clothesline and crackled in the wind. A wreath that had seen better days hung on the front door. Bobby climbed the steps and knocked while Al stood by the SUV. Two meowing cats came out of nowhere and wrapped themselves around Bobby's ankles. Shivering with cold, he was happy when Hannah DeGroot allowed them to enter the warm house with him.

"Sheriff Hanley! What brings you out here on Christmas Eve?"

Hannah was Vince and Edith Edna DeGroot's daughter. She was a horsey-looking woman with short cropped brown hair in no particular style. Bobby remembered her from last June when he'd questioned them about the disappearance of Harvey Johnson, Sr. She'd moved back from Bozeman, Montana, to take care of her mother who suffered from some form of dementia. Back in June, it had not been called Alzheimer's disease, but Bobby was pretty sure that was currently the official diagnosis. He remembered that Edith Edna offered him tea and cookies when he'd last been there, then came back into the living room carrying a tray covered with silverware. She offered the tray to Bobby and, not knowing what else to do, he'd taken a fork and smiled at her. What would that be like, he'd thought with sympathy for, not only Edith Edna, but also for Vince and their daughter, Hannah. Especially for Hannah, who must have given up her life to come back and be a nursemaid to her mother.

Hannah was only in her late thirties or early forties, but had aged since Bobby saw her last. She ushered him into the same living room where he'd sat six months earlier. The same map of Iowa above the TV showed ninety-nine counties in pastel colors. He sat down in the same worn leather recliner and was hit with the realization there was definitely a connection between the disappearance of Harvey Johnson and the missing horses. No one goes missing without a trace. Eight horses don't go missing without a trace. I just need to find that trace, he thought with a premonition that the DeGroots knew something. That feeling was very strong and getting stronger when he was suddenly aware of a new person in the room. He looked around and saw Edith Edna DeGroot standing in the doorway.

"Mother. Come. Sit." Hannah urged and motioned her mother toward the sofa. Edith Edna DeGroot was extremely thin and her bony shoulders poked through her faded red sweater. Her loose baggy jeans were held up by a frayed cloth belt, and her gray hair looked tangled but clean. A startling unhappiness filled her watery eyes. She didn't say anything or even acknowledge the stranger in her living room. Bobby stood and cleared his throat.

"Hello, Mrs. DeGroot. How are you?" Not getting any response, he turned to Hannah and got to the point of the visit. "Hannah, could I speak with your father?"

"He's not here, Sheriff."

"Do you know when he'll return?"

"No, no, I don't," she hesitated.

"I didn't see any tracks in your lane. Has he been gone overnight?"

She laughed without smiling. "I guess you could say that. He's been gone several months. We have no idea where he is. He got tired of all this." She nodded her head slightly toward her mother.

"I'm sorry to hear that." He paused. He glanced around the room. There was an afghan on the back of the sofa and a few framed family photos on the end tables. The lamps were shabby and the coffee table was covered with tattered magazines, but the room was warm and a small Christmas tree decorated with lights stood in the corner. "Do you need help, Hannah? There are places for people like…" he stopped. He did not want to offend this woman who seemed to be coping with what life had dealt.

"For people like my mother?" she asked.

"Yes, people with Alzheimer's. There are homes. I don't know all the details, but I can look into it for you." Bobby didn't know if the DeGroots had a savings account or if Hannah had some income, but he knew they were not living high on the hog.

"Thanks, Sheriff. For now, we're fine. We are," she said with certainty. "Now, maybe you'd like to tell me why you came out in this weather on Christmas Eve?"

Hanley started to explain about Harvey Johnson's missing horses. At some point, he and Hannah both sat down again, while Edith Edna stood and left the room as if she was bored with all the talking. Bobby could hear her in the kitchen and was distracted by a loud crash of breaking glass. Hannah jumped and excused herself. After a few minutes, Edith Edna wandered back into the room. Bobby stood and asked her if Hannah needed help.

"Help the horses."

"Pardon me. What did you say, Mrs. DeGroot?"

She looked blankly at Bobby's face. Hannah came running back into the room.

"Mother! Would you like to take a nap now?" Hannah was winded and, not waiting for a response, she ushered her mother out of the room. Bobby followed them as far as the open door and watched as Hannah helped her mother slowly down the hall. When she came back, Hannah apologized.

"No problem. Your mother said something to me though—something that sounded like, *help the horses*. What do you make of that? Do you own horses?"

"My mother has Alzheimer's, Sheriff. You can't put much stock in anything she says. She probably heard you talking about the missing horses. She loves horses, or used to anyway, but, no, we don't own any horses."

"Okay." He headed for the front door, and turned around when he got there. "You won't mind if my deputy and I search your outbuildings?" He hoped Al was keeping warm in the car but, when he opened the door, he saw Al walking toward one of the run-down sheds.

"You need a search warrant for that, don't you?" Hannah asked calmly.

"Hard to get a search warrant on Christmas Eve, Hannah, but this is just standard procedure. We're checking all Johnson's neighbors." He stressed the *all* but his gut told him they were right where they should be, and Hannah DeGroot was hiding something.

"Come back Monday with a warrant, and you can look anywhere you want. I need to get back to Mother now. Let us have

Christmas." She closed the door leaving Sheriff Hanley on the front step. He pulled his stocking cap down over his ears, and walked toward Al, who met him halfway between the car and the old shed.

"I heard a horse, Sheriff."

Wind swept through the trees and around the corner of the barn and they listened.

They heard nothing but the wind.

"The DeGroots don't own horses, Al, so if you did hear one, we need to look in that shed."

He wondered what Hannah meant. "Let us have Christmas."

Bobby pulled off a glove and looked at his watch. Noon already. He figured they had two choices. Phone the county attorney in Newtown and see if they could get a warrant, or decide that a horse whinny was probable cause to search the shed, and get it over with. He knew he should have phoned Mary Jo by now. She'd be wondering if they got home safely last night and how Scott and Tennille were doing. He noticed Al checking his watch and stamping his feet to keep warm.

"Do you have anything going on this afternoon, Al?"

"I'm supposed to pick up Kevin at the Nook at one when he gets off, but I can call him and tell him I'll be late."

The snow had stopped and Bobby realized they might be able to get the warrant and be back in an hour or two. He'd thought about having Al wait while he left for it, but he also knew if any horses were going to be moved out of that shed today, there would be plenty of tracks left in the snow as evidence. He looked back at the house and saw Hannah watching them.

"Come on," he motioned to Al. "Let's see what our favorite Jasper County attorney is doing on Christmas Eve."

They got back into the black unmarked SUV just as Sheriff Hanley's cell phone rang. It was Scott sounding odd, and Bobby had a sinking feeling.

"Dad. Where are you?"

"Over near Monroe looking for those missing horses. What's wrong?"

"It's Tennille. She's having labor pains we think. Dad, we think she's in labor. I'm not sure and I don't know what to do."

"Scott, has her water broke?"

Bobby listened to Scott talking with Tennille. He could hear panic in both their voices and then a scream.

"Scott, call 911. They'll take you to the medical center in town faster than I can get there, and I'll meet you there. Do what they tell you to do. I'm on my way, Son."

"But what if it's not actual labor? She isn't due for another month, Dad."

"Scott. Call 911 now. If it's a false alarm, it'll be okay. Just call 911. Now!" he yelled as he ended the call and maneuvered the snow-covered lane as fast as he safely could.

Before they reached Al's house, they decided that Al would call the county attorney and get a search warrant prepared for a judge's signature. Not knowing which district judge would be on call on the holiday, they both hoped it would be Assistant District Court Judge Carol Van Kooten. She'd read the warrant carefully and ask a few questions, but she was fast and efficient and wouldn't waste their time. Modest to a fault, she didn't believe in throwing her weight around. In Al's driveway, they wished each other luck and headed their separate ways—Bobby to the medical center in Newtown, and Al to get ahold of the county attorney.

Chapter 6

After lunch, I decided Archie could accompany us to the festivities. He loved being outside, and the boys loved his company. Ted and Cara bundled up the boys, and we all headed out to their minivan. The boys had fun seeing their breath turn to frost in the nippy air, and for a second I felt like a child, too, as I pursed my lips and blew out my breath. The snow had stopped and the sun was breaking through. We let Archie jump into the back, while the boys and I sat in the middle seat and listened to the snow crunch beneath the tires as we headed downtown to the square. City organizers had hung wreaths on all the lamp posts around the square where Sinter Klauss always made his appearance on Christmas Eve day along with two of his reindeer—real reindeer with antlers from the VanDerMeer family farm. There would be stands of cookies and hot chocolate, popcorn balls, and Dutch letters—an S-shaped pastry filled with almond paste. The first-place gingerbread house would be on display in the frosted, mullioned window of Jaarsma's Bakery, and I'd have a chance to duck into the Book Nook to see how Kevin was handling any last-minute shoppers.

When Noah and Max entered the snowman-building contest, I told Cara where I was headed and that I'd meet them back at the windmill just off the town square in an hour. I walked one block north to the shop on the other side of the square and stopped to admire the front window before I went in. The shop was empty except for Kevin, who was closing out the cash register, and Stella, who was sitting on the counter at Kevin's elbow batting her paw at the bills Kevin was counting. We always closed by one o'clock on Christmas Eve, and it was now closer to two.

Kevin looked up and smiled. He was a good kid. Between Al, who had taken Kevin in to live with him, and me, who hired him on a part-time basis at the Nook, Kevin was doing well. His grades were above average. He didn't give Al any trouble as a housemate, and he took good care of his dog, Catfish, and Stella, the Book Nook's resident cat.

"She's helping me count, Mary Jo," Kevin grinned.

I laughed and we started discussing the morning's business—smaller than I'd like, but decent considering the economy. We both turned when we heard the door open and boots stamping on the rug. It was Al, who had come to give Kevin a ride home. He pulled his stocking cap and aviator sunglasses off, rubbing his hand over his shaved head as he walked slowly toward me.

"Mrs. Mac," he exclaimed. "I'm glad you're here. I wanted to talk to you alone last night, but never got the chance. Your lasagna was well above average, by the way. Do you have a minute?" he asked quietly.

"I've got all the time in world. What's up?" I was curious. Al looked at Kevin and Kevin started to excuse himself.

"No, don't leave, Kev. It's no big secret. Not after tonight anyway." He pulled a small blue velvet box out of his down jacket pocket. "I want to marry Pippi, but I want your permission to ask her. She means so much to me, and I love her. You mean a lot to me, too, Mrs. Mac, and so I hope you will give us your blessing. I know she could do better, but I love her, and I'll always be good to her. I promise you I will. I have this ring for her."

He opened the box and a beautiful ring shone up at me. It wouldn't have mattered to me if it was beautiful or not. Al's little speech touched my heart. I'd known him for years, but it wasn't until he started dating Pippi that I'd gotten to really know him. He was a sweet and kind and gentle young man. Pippi's eyes lit up whenever she saw him, and I'd never seen her so happy as when she was with him. I grabbed him in the biggest bear hug possible.

"My permission? My blessing?" I asked with tears of joy streaming down my face. "You have both. You don't need them, but you have them. I'm so happy, Al. I can't tell you how happy. Everyone can see how much you two belong together." I fished for a tissue in my pocket and blew my nose. "I am so happy for you. I'm just so happy," I slobbered. We stood and talked until Kevin was ready to lock up. Al said he planned to propose to Pippi after midnight Mass tonight at St. Mary's.

"You're going, aren't you?"

"Um, I'm not sure. Cara and I haven't talked about it. The boys are too young to stay up that late, so I, uh, don't know," I hedged. Pippi and Cara both loved midnight Mass, but I had stopped going to church years ago for reasons of my own. "Maybe Ted and Cara and Pippi can all go while I stay home with the boys." I hadn't heard from Bobby all morning, so I wasn't sure what his plans were now that he had two houseguests of his own. What I was sure of was that this was not going to be the romantic Christmas Eve I had envisioned for Bobby and me. I decided to ask Al if he'd seen Bobby.

"Yes, ma'am. We were out looking for missing horses, but he got a call from Scott saying they thought Tennille was going into labor, so he dropped me off at home and headed back to Newtown." Al checked his watch. "That was just thirty-five minutes ago. Not sure the sheriff wants to be delivering his own grandchild on Christmas Eve. Not that he couldn't. I'm just not sure he'd want to. Well, who would?"

"Yes, who would?" I knew Bobby had delivered a baby or two during his tenure as a county deputy and then as sheriff, but if there were complications, I knew I'd want to be in a hospital instead of the back seat of some sheriff's car.

Tennille was so young. She must be scared stiff. Where did she say her parents lived? Should I call Bobby to see if I can help? I decided to wait. Something told me not to interfere. If Bobby needed help, he'd call me.

Then, Al told me he was in a hurry because he had to get a warrant signed. At least I knew why Bobby hadn't called me all morning. Naturally, Bobby would be with Scott and Tennille. After Al and Kevin left, my mind wandered back to Mass. When my ex-husband, Don, told me he was going to have our marriage annulled, I was surprised. We'd been divorced a couple of months, and although we'd always attended Mass on Sundays with the girls, I gradually stopped going. Ann and Cara were both married by then, and Pippi seemed content to stay home on Sunday mornings with me. We took hikes or played tennis in the summer. During the school year, she would have homework and I'd have papers to correct since I was a sociology instructor at the community college back then. Some days, she would go to Mass by herself, or attend the Dutch Reformed Church with friends. But, when Don had our marriage annulled, I felt betrayed by the Catholic Church. What right did it have to say our marriage never existed? And what did that make our children, if our marriage never existed? I realized annulments allowed the Church could keep congregants, but it didn't make sense to me. I was angry at Don, at the Church, and at myself, I suppose, but whatever the reason, I stopped attending Mass.

Now, I wanted to go. Something was pulling me in that direction, and it wasn't just Al. Al must have forgotten I'd stopped going, or maybe he just thought I needed an invitation to get me there. I loved going to midnight Mass on Christmas Eve with my family when I was a young, but those were childhood memories, and a lot has changed. I'm different. I still believe in "'til death do us part," but I believe there are other kinds of death than just physical death. There is emotional death and a spiritual death I felt when Don and I were divorced.

Archie's bark jostled me out of my reflection, and I jumped turning to see a customer peek his head through the door.

"Are you still open for a late shopper?" he asked.

He looked to be about my age and, although dressed for the cold weather, looked more like a visitor-from-New York type than a resident of Holland.

"Yes, come in out of the cold. I was just closing up, but you're welcome to look around. I can easily spend some time straightening up." Archie bounded over to the door and the man reached down to pet him.

"Nice dog. You must be the owner—of the shop, I mean, and, the dog too?" I smiled and nodded. Wait until he spots the cat sleeping in the armchair, I thought. I wondered why Kevin hadn't taken Stella home with him. It didn't matter really. She liked the shop just fine, but I wasn't sure I'd want to come in on Christmas Day tomorrow just to feed her. I made a mental note to call Kevin to see if he'd come get her.

"I'm sorry to be so late, but I just realized I need a new book to get me through the holidays. Any suggestions?" He stood up from petting Archie. He was about six feet tall and thin. He removed his tweed newsboy cap. How is it some men never get hat hair? His hair was thick and gray and curly and he had a massive dark gray mustache. Black rimmed eyeglasses and a plaid neck scarf gave him a professorial air. Bingo! I was pretty sure my customer was a professor at Central College.

"What do you teach?" I ventured.

"Ha. Is it that obvious?"

"No." I said too quickly, suddenly thinking it might be a bad thing to guess someone's occupation by his looks. "Well, yes." I corrected. "You haven't been in the store before, that I know of anyway, and you must live in Holland, or why would you be here shopping on Christmas Eve? You're clearly not a farmer. I know most of the people who work downtown, which means you work outside of town, maybe at the college. I'll wait to see what book you pick out before I go any further." I laughed.

"Ah, a detective. But, I could be visiting someone in Holland and found myself short a gift."

"But, you already said you needed a book to get *you* through the holidays."

"That I did. That I did." He stopped smiling at me and turned sober. "Can you help me find something? I like poetry, but I'd also like a page-turner." I had started to wander over to the small poetry section and he followed. He pulled Mary Oliver's latest off the shelf, and I pulled Charles Baudelaire. He looked at it in my hands and took it from me. "My favorite. How did you know?"

"I didn't," I stuttered. "Just a lucky guess, I guess. I'll point you to the mystery section, but if you haven't read any Lee Child books, they are definitely page-turners. They're the Jack Reacher books," I said excitedly. "And, my newest favorite mystery writer is Louise Penny. She lives in Quebec and that is the setting of her mystery series. She throws in a little French, too, to keep us on our toes. Do you speak any French?"

"Bien sur, madame. Et vous?"

"Oui. Mais tres peu."

"You have a lovely accent. I teach languages at Central, by the way." He raised Baudelaire's book to show me. "I'll like this very much. I don't have this one. I'll also try Mademoiselle Penny. Or, is it Madame Penny?"

"I believe Madame Penny is married." Too late I realized I had glanced at my wristwatch and he noticed it.

"I'm so sorry. I've taken up too much of your time." He apologized. Thirty minutes had passed quickly, but now I needed to hurry back to the kids.

"No, no." I protested. "This was fun. I'm glad you found something." I rang up the sale. He stooped to pet Archie again, and soon he was gone after promising to return and let me know how he liked the two new authors I recommended. The charge slip told me his name was Oliver Burns. *Nice man*, I mused, and wondered if I'd see him again.

By the time Archie and I'd locked up and met the kids back at the windmill, the sky was turning dark. It looked like it would start snowing again. The boys were jumping up and down, excited to have won candy canes for their snowman-building contest, so we all headed over to the square to see the kids' efforts. Ted whispered to me that all the children "won" candy canes. I laughed and then oohed and aahed when I saw Max and Noah's attempt. I used my most businesslike tone and asked if they used my neighbor, Joe, as their model because it really did resemble Noni's husband. "Where ever did you find the sunglasses and seed corn cap?" I asked Max.

"In our car. Dad said we could use them." Max shouted.

"Well, I love it! It's definitely the best snowman here!" I spun around looking at the other snowmen. "I'm so proud of you both. Now, is anyone hungry?"

With shouts of "yes, yes" and "I'm thirsty," we raced to the car. I wondered about Bobby and how things were going with Tennille at the hospital. I'd absent-mindedly left my cell phone at home and was hoping for a message from him when we got back.

The boys were rosy-cheeked and tired from their outdoor activities and headed for the TV. Cara started making hot chocolate, and I checked the answering machine and my cell phone. No message from Bobby on either. I felt disappointment rise up in me and, if I was being honest with myself, I felt downright neglected and wondered if my feelings were warranted. He was on duty after all and was trying to track down missing horses, and his son's girlfriend was in the hospital giving birth. The man was having a busy day, so I stifled my feelings and got on with my own family. If he didn't call by dinnertime, I decided I'd give him a call. Just as we were sitting down to our hot casserole dinner, the kitchen phone rang. I jumped to get it.

"Mom, Al and I are going to midnight Mass and want to know if we can pick you up. Al said you might like to go."

My heart sank. I'd thought for sure it was Bobby.

"No, I don't think so, Pippi. Cara and Ted are going and, I offered to stay with the boys. We're going to watch a movie on TV and make popcorn. And anyway, I'll be pretty worn out by then. Frankly, I'm a little worn out already so go on without me. Just be sure to come over in the morning for brunch before Cara and Ted leave."

"Okay, but we might be a little late. What time do you plan on letting the boys open their gifts? Is anyone else coming?"

"Well, no, I don't think so. Like who?"

"Like Bobby?"

"Oh. I don't know. I haven't heard from him all day. Al said they were busy and then, of course, Tennille's possibly giving birth. So..." my voice trailed off.

"Mom, call him. Find out what's going on with Tennille and let us know what you find out. Gotta run. See you tomorrow around ten. Call Bobby!"

That's when I decided I would call Bobby as soon as we were finished eating dinner.

"Bobby? Are you still at the hospital? What's happening?"

"Mary Jo. Hi! You won't believe this. Tennille just had a baby girl. She came a little early. She weighs four pounds and ten ounces. The doc says that's a good weight considering how early she is. They tried to stop the contractions, but I guess that baby has a mind of her own. She's beautiful, Red. Truly beautiful. I can't wait for you to see her." Bobby was speaking softly, maybe because he was in a hospital, but my heart was telling me he was in awe of what he'd just experienced—the birth of his first grandchild. And, he wanted me to see her.

"That's wonderful, Bobby. I'm so happy for you. Are you okay? How's Tennille doing?"

"Haven't seen her yet. She had a difficult time, I guess. Scott is in with her now. I'm just waiting around for him to come out. Kinda hate to leave, but there really isn't any reason for me to stay unless you'd like to come over and see the baby."

"Now?" I asked. I couldn't really leave, could I? Maybe I didn't want to leave my family on Christmas Eve to see Bobby's new grandchild. I felt torn. The roads weren't good, and we'd planned on playing games with the boys before bedtime. "No, I really can't leave with Ted and Cara here, and they're planning on me watching the boys while they go to midnight Mass to-night. But, Bobby, you could come over here and spend the night. The boys and I are going to play Pictionary and Uno, but they'll be in bed by eight-thirty or nine."

"Ah, sorry, Mary Jo. It's been a long day. I don't think I could stay awake for games. Can you get along without me?"

I assured him I could, and he hung up after promising to come for brunch in the morning. I knew Ted and Cara planned to leave for Omaha and their own Christmas right after brunch. In fact, the little boys were told Santa would be delivering their gifts a little late this year, but would surely be in Omaha by Christmas morning.

I figured we could drive over to Newtown to see Bobby's new granddaughter after Ted and Cara left. Bobby had sounded tired, but happy. Happier than I'd heard him sound in a while. Did he even remember that we'd planned on spending Christmas Eve together at my house? I looked at his present under the tree and our favorite Christmas CDs stacked by the player. It would all wait until tomorrow, of course, but my romantic Christmas Eve with Bobby was definitely put on the back burner. Instead of showering and opening a bottle of wine, I busied myself with throwing my eggs Benedict casserole together for tomorrow's brunch.

As soon as Bobby hung up, he punched in Al's cell phone number.

"Congratulations, Sheriff! Pippi just told me the news."

"Thanks, Al. But, what did you find out today? Were you able to get a warrant?" He yawned.

"Negative. County Attorney Van Vleet said a horse whinnying in a barn is not probable cause because there is nothing unusual about a horse whinnying in a farmer's barn. She said to come back Monday with proof from neighbors that the DeGroots don't own horses."

"That's okay, Al. I know you tried."

"Affirmative, Sheriff."

"I don't think Hannah DeGroot is going to move any horses on Christmas Day."

"So you think those stolen horses are in her barn? Really?"

"I think there's a good chance. If you say you heard a horse, Al, I know you heard a horse. I need to go. Scott needs to talk to me before I head home."

"Roger that. Merry Christmas, Sheriff."

"Merry Christmas, Al."

Chapter 7

After the boys finally settled down for the night, the house suddenly fell overwhelmingly silent. I imagined I could hear snow falling. I walked through the house shutting off all the lights except one for Ted and Cara's return. Lastly, I pulled the plug on the Christmas tree. Archie came up behind me and nuzzled his nose on my leg. We walked to the back porch, and he lunged into the snow when I opened the door. It was beautiful outside—one of those nights when the moon shines bright and everything is covered with snow making it eerily like daytime. The trees mimicked charcoal drawings against a white canvas. They'd lost their leaves, and snow lay in a thin line on the branches. I let Archie play for a few minutes while I savored the moment, and then called him in. He shook snow all over the porch, and I shivered as I locked the door.

"Come on, Arch. Bedtime."

I woke dreaming that I had fallen through an ice-covered lake and was drowning. My lungs were frozen and I couldn't breathe. As I thrashed my way to the surface, I realized the frozen lake was just my heavy quilt holding me down. The room was dark and the clock on my nightstand said four a.m. I untangled myself from the quilt and got out of bed. I hopped across the cold tiles in the dark bathroom. When I crawled back into bed, I knew I wouldn't get back to sleep. My head was not filled with sugarplums but with thoughts of Bobby and how much I was missing him. Sleet was making pebble noises against the window. I hadn't heard Ted and Cara come in after church last night, but assumed they did. I decided to go upstairs to check anyway. They were sound asleep in the guest bedroom and one of the boys had crawled into bed with them. The other one was still asleep on the bunk bed in Pippi's old room. I headed back downstairs to the kitchen to make some tea and toast.

Al and Pippi brought Kevin to brunch. They all looked like they needed a little more sleep, and I knew I could have used an extra hour or two. The little boys were excited from opening their gifts and acted like Kevin was closer to their age than the adults' ages. Kevin played along taking turns running their remote cars. They'd met Kevin last summer in the Book Nook and were enamored with him. Since then, they'd asked their mom almost daily when they could see Kevin again.

Kevin has a dog named Catfish.

Kevin knows how to fish.

Kevin plays basketball and is the best one on the whole team.

Kevin said this. Kevin said that.

Cara told us she got so tired of hearing how wonderful Kevin was, she told the boys not to tell Kevin how great he is. "It will go straight to his head," she said, "and then he'll think too much of himself and become a mean person."

"Well, what was I supposed to tell them?" she asked in her defense, as she filled glasses with orange juice and cranberry juice. Then, she screamed and dropped the plastic juice bottle. "Pippi! Al! You guys! Why didn't you tell me? Let me see it!" She hardly needed to ask to see the ring because Pippi was holding it right under Cara's nose. Ted congratulated Al and Pippi while Cara was torn between mopping spilled juice off the floor and asking Pippi if they'd set a date. "When did Al propose? Were you surprised? Mom, did you know about this?"

"Al told me yesterday. He actually asked for my permission."

Whoops of good-natured kidding made Al blush. I smiled and looked at the clock wondering what was keeping Bobby. As though I'd conjured him up, he walked through the side door looking as tired as everyone else.

"Merry Christmas, everyone. Sorry I'm late." He gave me a quick kiss and kicked off his boots, still holding a large gift-wrapped box, which Al grabbed and put next to the Christmas tree. Soon, everyone was congratulating him on becoming a grandpa and asking Al and Pippi when they were going to tie the knot.

When everyone was finished eating, Cara and Ted packed up their van. The boys begged to stay until they were reminded of more gifts at home. We all waved goodbye from the front porch, and then Pippi and I slowly started cleaning up the kitchen mess. Bobby and Al and Kevin got comfortable in the living room, and I could hear them talking to Archie. Soon their voices changed from "cute dog" talk to "missing horses" talk. I definitely wanted to hear more about the horses, so I went in and asked if they'd like a cup of tea.

"Is there any coffee left?" Bobby asked.

"Coffee? You don't drink coffee, do you?" I asked.

"Well, I'm not a Mormon." Bobby and Al both laughed. Kevin looked at me. As my employee, he has never seen me bear the brunt of a joke. He had the good sense not to laugh.

"Ah, no, but I've never seen you drink coffee either," trying to keep the hurt out of my voice.

"Anything is fine with me, Mary Jo. Here, let me get it," Bobby said and then added, "You look tired."

I absolutely hate being told I looked tired. I equated it with, "My, you look old." However, I was tired so I sat down on the sofa next to Al. Bobby returned with a cup of hot coffee. "Anyone else need anything as long as I'm up?" he asked. Kevin still had a can of pop, and Al declined. I lifted my mug of tea and said I was fine. I was curious to see if they'd talk shop in front of me. Much to my amazement, they did after a full minute of silence while Bobby sipped his coffee.

"There's got to be a connection between those horses and the disappearance of Harvey Johnson, Sr. The DeGroot and Johnson properties back up to each other, and Hannah DeGroot was hiding something yesterday. She said they hadn't heard from her father in about six months. That would be about the same time Johnson went missing. That cannot be just a coincidence, Al. We'll drive out there again in the morning and see if we find anything that might validate a warrant."

"I'll be ready. What time are you going to pick me up?" Al paused. "Two missing people. Missing horses. Either one of the Johnsons or one of the DeGroot women or both, know something and I'm betting it's Hannah DeGroot, the daughter. Did you see the way she watched us out the window as we were leaving yesterday—like something out of a scary movie?"

"Well, her mother isn't going to be much help, Al. Not if she really does have Alzheimer's, and I think that's pretty much a fact." He leaned forward on the sofa and ran both hands through his short blond-gray hair. "We've been thinking that Harvey Johnson is a victim, but maybe Vince DeGroot is a victim, too. Or, maybe DeGroot knows something. Let's do a missing person search for Vince DeGroot. See if Jamie can run one first thing in the morning, and, some time I want to talk with Junior's wife, Jean."

I'd been sitting silently listening to the conversation. Kevin had gotten up and was helping Pippi in the kitchen. My curiosity was aroused, and I *had* helped Bobby solve a murder case last June after all.

"Where do these DeGroots live?" I asked and waited for Bobby's warning to stay out of their business. He and Al both looked over at me. I took a sip of my tea which had gotten cold.

"They live off County Road A47 out of Monroe about two miles. Their farm backs up to the Johnsons' farm on B10. That's one reason we think there is a connection between the missing horses and the missing Harvey Johnson, Sr," Bobby said matter-of-factly.

At that moment, I knew something had changed between Bobby and me. I knew he was tired, but I also knew he used to worry about my involvement in his cases. Now, it seemed he no longer cared if I went snooping. That is why I was not shocked when, later that day, he told me his plan.

Bobby was the first to leave. Said he was anxious to get to the hospital to see how Tennille and the new baby were doing. He offered to take me also, but I wanted to help Pippi finish cleaning up the kitchen. Al and Pippi wanted to see the baby, too, so they offered to drive me over to Newtown after dropping Kevin off at home. We all agreed it was a plan, and I was glad I'd accepted the ride with Al, because after we dropped Kevin off, Al confided in me that Kevin's grades had dropped. I was surprised, but felt a little guilty. With Christmas and spending more hours at the Book Nook, I knew I'd probably neglected Kevin. He'd started playing college basketball, and maybe it was all too much for him along with his part-time job working for me at the Nook.

Al thought that basketball practices were taking up much of Kevin's time, but felt it was important for Kevin to succeed in a team sport for the first time in his young life. I agreed but I knew

Kevin needed the money he was making at the Nook to help pay for books and tuition. I suggested I cut his hours to just two afternoons a week during basketball season. I would put a Help Wanted sign in my window the next day, and Al said he'd be more diligent in making sure Kevin studied every evening.

"I can help with that, too," Pippi said. "Even though I teach middle school, it doesn't mean I don't know what college kids need to up their grades. Al, you and I are going to be a team. You can be the coach and I'll be your assistant. Mom, don't worry about Kevin. Just see if you can get some extra help at the Nook during basketball season. When the season's over, Kevin could come back full-time. Right?"

When we pulled into the visitor parking lot at the hospital fifteen minutes later, we felt good about our plan to help Kevin. Some of the parking lot had been cleared of snow, but we were glad we wore boots as we climbed over a mound of snow near the front sidewalk. We stomped on the huge black mat inside so we didn't leave sloppy puddles all over the lobby and elevator. The lobby was decorated from floor to ceiling with tinsel and tiny colored lights. Christmas music played joyfully, and nurses wore green and red patterned smocks.

I heard Bobby's quiet voice as we entered Tennille's room on the second floor. He stood at the side of the bed and was holding his new sleeping granddaughter in his arms. He looked up at us and grinned. He held the baby tenderly and gently, yet confidently, reminding me of a running back with a football. I grinned back at him and walked over to get a closer look. He gave me a peck on my cheek.

"Merry Christmas," he whispered in my ear.

"Merry Christmas, Grandpa," I replied giving a peck on his cheek. He smelled of soap and pine and I breathed in the scent. I had missed him the last two nights.

The baby was beautiful. She had dark hair like Tennille and there was a lot of it

"Have you named her?" Pippi asked.

"Noelle," replied Tennille sitting up in bed looking like someone who had not just given birth, and a difficult birth at that. Her makeup appeared professionally applied. Her short haircut styled with precision. I glanced quickly in the mirror at my windblown mop and weather-reddened cheeks and silently groaned.

Of course, they would name a baby girl born on Christmas Eve Noelle, I thought. It's a pretty name, really. Tennille swung her legs out from under the covers. She was drowning in someone's large gray sweat pants and a hospital issued cotton robe. I vowed to ask Pippi if she had any "girl" clothes that Tennille might borrow. Tennille's bare feet looked like they were freezing because her toenails were polished dark purple. I wished I'd thought to bring her some slippers. She reached her arms out for the baby, and Bobby started to hand her over, but not before brushing the dark hair off the infant's forehead and giving her a kiss. He whispered something to her ending with *angel*, and then handed her to Tennille. I admired this soft side of Bobby and had seen it many times. Not all men openly display affection, but Bobby never hesitated to give a person in need a hug or arm around a shoulder. Scott stayed sitting in a recliner in the corner of the room. He was friendly to us. He just didn't seem to know he should get up and offer one of us a seat.

We all chatted and, although we were curious as to Scott and Tennille's plans, no one asked. As far as I knew, Scott still had a job waiting for him in Las Vegas and wasn't too keen on visiting our sleepy town of Holland any longer than necessary. When the baby woke up and started to cry, a nurse came in and told Tennille it was time to feed baby Noelle. We took that as our cue to leave. I was glad Bobby left with us. We walked to the elevator and when we exited Bobby offered to drive me home.

"I still haven't given you your present yet, Red. Careful!" He grabbed my arm as I slipped on some ice.

"Nor I, yours," I smiled cagily. I shivered in the frigid wind and stepped into deep snow. Snow plows continued to clear the lot.

"I have a granddaughter, Mary Jo. I can't really believe it yet. Is she as beautiful as I think she is?" he asked as we climbed over the mound of snow. He directed me toward his car.

"She is, Bobby. She's beautiful. So tiny. And that hair!"

We got into his Pathfinder and headed to my house with the heater and fan turned on high. For not seeing each other much in the last three days, we hardly talked. I knew the loud fan wasn't the only reason for the silence. I could tell Bobby was preoccupied, and I assumed it was because of Scott and Tennille and his new granddaughter, or possibly the stolen horses and missing man.

As we pulled into my driveway, I noticed Joe and Noni's kids had all departed. I could see the blue TV screen through their front window, and I knew Noni felt the same letdown I always experienced when my kids left after a long visit. Especially on Christmas. I was glad I had Bobby. Glad he seemed to be free for the rest of the day. Barring an emergency, of course.

We pulled off our coats and boots, and I quickly let a tail-wagging Archie out into the backyard. It was about four o'clock and starting to get dark. The sky was cloudless and dark gray.

"Are you hungry? We have a ton of leftovers, or should we open our gifts to one another?" I babbled feeling a little strange. I'd been upset for two days because of Scott and Tennille's sudden appearance in Holland that had taken Bobby away from me and disrupted our plans, but now he was here, and I couldn't let myself feel grateful. Something was not right.

"Let's just relax for a few minutes. It's been quite a day—quite a weekend really." He plopped down on the sofa breathing a sigh of relief. He dropped his head into his hands and ran his fingers through his slightly graying hair. He looked up at me and said, "Come here. Let's talk," motioning me to sit beside him.

I had a premonition and offered to get us a glass of wine, or something else to drink to delay hearing whatever Bobby wanted to talk about. He was acting much too serious. I knew in my being that this would have something to do with Scott, and I was right.

"Mary Jo, I don't know how to say this, so I'll just say it. Scott asked me to move to Las Vegas with him when I retire in June, and I think I would really like to do that."

My mouth dropped open. Now, I knew what the word "speechless" meant.

"Really?" I finally asked. I looked at his tired face for clues. "Are you teasing me? You're kidding, right? Las Vegas. You think you'd like living in Las Vegas?"

He smiled and told me how he and Sharon had visited Las Vegas before she died and they'd liked it, and how he'd visited Scott a few times in the past few years and loved the fishing and the hiking in the mountains. The warmer weather. Even the casinos.

"Mountains? What mountains? You liked the casinos?" I asked incredulously. I got up and walked over to the front window and looked out into the twilight. The streetlights had come on and swayed a little in the wind. Cold air seeped in around the window, and I shivered. I turned around to face Bobby.

He said he didn't remember the name of the mountains, but there were mountains, maybe the Spring Mountains, he thought. He told me how he'd been thinking of moving somewhere when he retired, and now that he had a granddaughter, he'd like to be close enough to watch her grow up. That was certainly something I could relate to, but still, all I could think about was, what about us? What about Bobby and me? I had to ask.

"I thought you were thinking of your cabin and Lake Eleanor in Minnesota, not moving a thousand miles away from here. What about me, Bobby? Don't you want to be near me?" I sat back down next to him.

He took my hands in his. "Of course, Red. Yes, I do want to be near you. Always. You know that, don't you? These past few months have been the happiest of my life," he paused, "that I can remember anyway. I love you, Red. That's why I want you to come to Las Vegas with me."

"Wh, wh, wh, well, I can't." I stuttered. "I can't leave Holland. I love it here. I love everything about this town—its Old

World charm and its friendly people. I love my home. I love Joe and Noni next door, and being close to Pippi. I'm even close enough to Chicago and Omaha to visit Ann and Cara whenever I want. What about the Nook, Bobby. I love the Book Nook. And the prairie. I can't just up and leave my work at the refuge. I can't leave." I shook my head from side to side. "No. I'm sorry."

I got up and went to the kitchen looking for the wine. I could hear Bobby in the living room starting a fire in the fireplace.

Maybe Bobby hasn't thought his plan through. Maybe he's in some sort of ecstatic dilemma about having a first grandchild. Wanting to be close to her. Not thinking straight. Doesn't sound like the Bobby I know, or maybe the Bobby I think I know.

He came out into the kitchen and took the wine bottle from my shaking hands and started to remove the cork.

"I shouldn't have sprung it on you so suddenly, Mary Jo. We could fly out there for a visit, and just see if you still feel the same way. You know, you might like it. And there is a wildlife refuge in Las Vegas, you know. It's not the Neal Smith, but it's good. I know you'd like it."

"You don't know. I've been there, Bobby. I hated it. It's like a fake town. Like the resorts and casinos are made of plywood and if one got blown down, all the rest would follow like Dominoes. That's how I saw Las Vegas. The lawns don't even have grass, for cryin' out loud, and I've read there is always a water shortage." I opened the refrigerator door and started taking out small containers of leftovers.

"I was talking about the refuge, Mary Jo. I know you'd like the refuge, and I think the desert is exotic, but maybe you just don't like exotic." Bobby teased.

"Dubai is exotic. Istanbul is exotic. Las Vegas is gaudy."

No response. I knew I was ruining another planned evening with just Bobby and me, but I didn't care. I was shocked at his idea of moving to Las Vegas. I realized he was serious, and I knew I was convincing him I would never move to Las Vegas, with him or with anybody. I remembered Archie was outside, and I went out to the back porch to let him in. He was leaping around in the snow and ignored my calls. That was another thing. Archie would hate Las Vegas, too, but I decided I didn't need to bring that up right now.

It didn't surprise me when I woke up snarled in the sheets and quilt. What did surprise me was that I'd fallen asleep at all. My mind was in turmoil. The evening had gone badly. I'd ruined our Christmas evening alone together. Oh, I'd warmed up the leftover casserole from the night before, and we made a salad together while sipping wine. We agreed we would let Las Vegas sit for awhile, but neither one of us could think of much else to talk about. We ate our dinner in silence like an old married couple.

I'd wanted to buy Bobby a rod and reel for fishing in Minnesota for his gift, but now I was glad that I hadn't. There were so many varieties and sizes in the store, I got confused and had left empty-handed. I ended up getting him a warm Irish wool cardigan and the latest Bill Bryson book. Now, I realized he would not need the warm sweater in Las Vegas, so I let his gifts sit under the tree. He must have been disillusioned with his choice of a gift for me also, because he never gave it to me. He simply told me it was a suitcase with four wheels that made it easier for pulling through airports. No doubt he thought we might be flying back and forth to Las Vegas. I felt like a character in O. Henry's "Gift of the Magi." Little did I know that inside the suitcase was a new smart phone, also. Maybe Bobby was covering his bases—a suitcase if I wanted to move to Las Vegas, and a new iPhone for long distance conversations if I didn't.

And then Bobby left. No hug or kiss good-bye. The one night we could have spent together was not to be. I heard my heart breaking.

"But Scott will probably stay at the hospital with Tennille tonight, Bobby. There's no need for you to drive home tonight." I tried not to plead.

"Sure, sure, I know, but I think it best if I go home. I'm sorry, Mary Jo. I'm worn out and have a full day tomorrow. Call me when you want to talk."

I started to cry as I closed the door behind him. I knew he was angry with me, but I was angry, too. The idea that I would move to Las Vegas with Bobby was just absurd. Archie whined and nuzzled my leg. Christmas carols still playing on the CD player only increased my frustration. I punched the off button, and started to clean up the kitchen. Then, I did what anyone else would do in that situation. I called my best friend.

"Noni? Am I interrupting anything?"

Noni listened to my tale of woe and offered to come over to comfort me some more, but I didn't want an eighty-three year old woman navigating the icy sidewalk between our houses for my benefit. I told her how I felt about casinos and the tourists and the glitz of Las Vegas.

"You probably wouldn't be living right on the Strip, Mary Jo," she said in her deadpan way.

I glanced out the window at Joe and Noni's house. Huge snowflakes were falling heavily like a white stage curtain. I could barely make out their house and their black roof was now covered in white. The pine trees looked like they'd been flocked. Every branch and needle was white. It was lovely really. Would Bobby miss the beautiful snowfalls if he moved away?

"It doesn't matter where I'd be living, Noni. I can't move away from here. I love it here."

"But, you love Bobby too. You'll have to decide what you want to do if Bobby does move out there. Is it a for sure thing, or is he just thinking about it?"

"I don't know. He sounded pretty sure. I know he feels guilty about never spending enough time with Scott while he was growing up, and he feels somewhat responsible for the trouble Scott was always getting into after Sharon died. And, now, there's Noelle."

"Who?"

"Oh! You don't know. Tennille had a baby girl yesterday and they named her Noelle because she was born on Christmas Eve. She's beautiful. We all went over there to see her this afternoon. She has Tennille's dark hair and lots of it. She's so tiny."

Noni and I talked on and on about our Christmas and our kids and grandkids and how much food we both had leftover. I told her I planned to drive to Anamosa tomorrow afternoon to visit Killian in prison. Of course, it depended on the weather and the roads, I'd said. I was feeling better when we hung up, and I had it in my head that I'd drive to Anamosa no matter what the weather. I felt sure Bobby wouldn't miss me. First I'd need to spend the morning at the Book Nook until Kevin showed up for his afternoon shift. I'd have the Help Wanted sign in the window by then and hoped he'd be happy to have his hours cut. It was exciting to think of hiring new help.

Chapter 8

Even before they entered, they heard the sound of hooves fitfully stamping on the frozen floor of the barn. Snorting. Whinnying. Al slid back the large roller-hung door. They stood waiting for their eyes to adjust from the bright white landscape to the dark and dusky barn interior, and then they saw them. Chestnut and black shiny backs. Spotted brown and white quivering rumps. Two were in steel pens and the other six were untethered in the open arena. Bobby and Al stepped cautiously inside.

"Close the door, Al."

"Wow! They're beautiful."

"They are." Bobby stepped closer and breathed in the smell of the horses—their skin, their breath, clean straw. He looked at Al. "Know anything about horses?"

"Not much, but look. They have hay for bedding. Sacks of feed over there," he pointed to a corner. He walked slowly toward the one with a bridle. "This one's clean and has been brushed. They all look like they've been brushed, Sheriff. See? It's dirty in here but there's no dust on the horses' backs."

Bobby stepped forward and approached one of the horses. It nuzzled Bobby's face knocking his sheriff's hat to the ground. A cat pounced out of nowhere and attacked the hat.

"Shoo!" Bobby scolded while picking up his hat.

"Sheriff. Look." Al pointed to one of the horses in a pen, its mane plaited with red and green ribbons. They both walked over for a closer look. The horse was skittish and backed up in fear. "Looks like we found the missing horses. Now what?"

Bobby thought for a minute. "We need to talk to Hannah." He spun around and slid the door back just enough for both of them to get out. He hadn't foreseen this. Hadn't really suspected Hannah of stealing horses. Was she even capable? How did she manage it? And why? Had he been so preoccupied with Scott and Tennille's visit and thoughts of moving to Las Vegas that he'd missed something? Mary Jo had been on his mind all morning. He knew he'd handled things badly with her the night before, and he'd wanted to call her first thing this morning, but barely had time to get to the office and pick up the warrant before meeting Al at DeGroots' farm. Al wandered across the snow-blanketed farmyard to a tank of some sort. It held water and blue balls.

"It's an automatic waterer. I'm guessing for the horses. See how these balls can be pushed down with their noses triggering the heater to keep the water from freezing." They looked around them seeing the stamped down snow around the waterer and dark horse droppings scattered in the snow. "At least they've taken good care of the horses, Sheriff. That's one good thing."

Bobby knew what Al said was true, and he was grateful the horses were found and in good condition, but, why were they taken by a close neighbor and what was the connection to the missing man, Harvey Johnson, Sr.? Hannah DeGroot's father went missing about the same time. Was that just coincidence? Bobby had heard of stranger things. Johnson was missing without a trace—gone up in proverbial smoke. Maybe he chose to go missing. Hard to declare suicide with no body. DeGroot was never reported as missing so there was no way to know if a crime had been committed, and hopefully, he could and would be found. Bobby told Al to check with Jamie to see if she'd found anything yet on Vince DeGroot.

He needed to let Harvey Junior know the horses were found and safe, but first he wanted to talk to Hannah DeGroot. He hoped she'd be forthcoming with information, because he sure didn't want to take her into jail to be questioned. He didn't know if her mother could be left alone.

As they approached the DeGroots' front door and climbed the steps, Bobby sensed something was wrong. He didn't know what it was, but he'd felt it two days ago when he questioned Hannah. This time, the feeling was stronger. Something wasn't adding up, and he knew he was overlooking something.

"Mornin', Sheriff. What can I do ya for?" Hannah stood with both hands behind her back. Her mother stood in the kitchen doorway behind Hannah. Bobby sensed that Al already had his hand on his holstered pistol.

"Show me your hands, Hannah. Slowly."

She slowly moved her hands to the front of her and raised them above her head in a surrender motion.

"Like this, Sheriff?" she grinned.

Bobby breathed relief, but tried not to show it. Could she be insane? He handed her the warrant to read, but she didn't take it from him.

"We searched your barn, Hannah. I think we can assume the eight horses in there are the Johnsons' missing horses." He still stood in the open doorway while Hannah shivered in a loose cotton shirt and the same brown corduroy slacks she'd worn last Friday. She did not invite them in. "Can we come in? I have a few questions for you."

She motioned them inside and led them down the hallway to the kitchen. Her mother stood aside and let them pass. Bobby smelled Edith Edna's unwashed hair and noticed the food stains on her sweater as he walked past her. The horses had appeared cleaner and better kept. Two women on their own, one with Alzheimer's. Were they capable of stealing horses? One couldn't do it on her own. It would take both of them. Bobby knew that when two people committed a crime, it was never a perfect crime. Two people couldn't keep a secret. Two would turn against each other. He needed to talk to Hannah and her mother separately. This wasn't difficult to manage. Hannah led Bobby to the kitchen, while her mother turned into the living room.

"Al, if it's all right with Hannah, would you sit and visit with Mrs. DeGroot while I talk to Hannah?" Hannah visibly tensed and took too long to reply.

"It's okay by me, Sheriff, as long as you don't ask her any questions. She's easily upset. You might even scare her." Hannah motioned to the mirror in the hallway which was covered with a bed sheet. "She's even scared of her own reflection in the mirror. That's why it's covered. She gets scared of the strangers on the TV, too. So please don't upset her." She put air quotes around *strangers* and gave Bobby a knowing look. He didn't have any personal experience with Alzheimer's, but was now imagining what it must be like caring for a victim of the disease.

"I won't, ma'am. I'll just sit and visit if she wants to visit. If she wants to just sit, that's fine with me," Al said.

Hannah and Sheriff Hanley walked down the hallway into the kitchen and sat at the retro red and silver chrome table strewn with newspapers, magazines, and grocery store coupons. Hannah didn't offer refreshments, which was fine with Bobby.

"Hannah, do you want to tell me how Harvey Johnson's horses came to be in your barn?"

"No."

"No, you don't want to tell me or no you don't know how they came to be in your barn?"

"It's not my barn, Sheriff. It's my father's barn. You should be asking him."

"But, he's not here is he? You said he disappeared about six months ago. Now, that's about the same time Harvey Johnson, Sr., went missing. Do you know anything about that?"

"No, I don't and if I did I wouldn't say. You seem more concerned about those horses than you do about my missing father."

"You never reported your father missing, Hannah. We would have searched for him. We still can search for him. As a matter of fact, I have an officer doing a search on the Internet. Do you have any idea where he might be? Would he be visiting someone? An old friend or a relative?" Bobby began listening not only to what Hannah was saying, but also to what she wasn't saying. He knew people often tried to hide the truth with short answers, but the truth often came out of the silences.

Hannah laughed, but couldn't cover up the surprised look in her eyes when Bobby said he'd begun a search for her father. He knew forty years of interviewing suspects made him good at obtaining the truth. A long time had passed since he'd outgrown shiny badge syndrome—when law enforcers overreacted with power and control, rather than insight and integrity.

"My dad didn't have friends. He has a sister in Oregon who hasn't had anything to do with him since their parents died."

"Was your father depressed?"

"No."

"Did he ever leave for a long period of time before?"

"No."

"Did he have money?"

"He cleaned out Mom's savings account and left her with nothing. I don't know if he had any other money," she said obscurely.

"A car?"

"He took their car. A Ford Taurus. White."

"What year?"

"Um, it had to be about five or six years old, I think." Hannah yawned.

"Okay." Bobby was getting frustrated. Hannah had seemed concerned about her father's absence, but not enough to cooperate with his questioning. He wanted to get back to the horses in her barn, but also was beginning to think Vince DeGroot might be involved in stealing the horses. If so, Vince might know something about the missing Harvey Johnson. "Does your father have a passport?"

"I don't know, but I doubt it. He wasn't much for traveling."

His cell phone rang. It was Jamie from the county jail office with the results of her search for Vince DeGroot. She told Bobby that DeGroot had no record, no previous arrests, and no history of mental illness. She told him DeGroot's driver's license expired over a year ago and was not renewed. There were three Vincent DeGroots listed on the Internet, but only one was in his seventies.

"Hannah, what's your father's middle name?" Bobby asked. When Hannah replied that his middle name was Albert, Bobby relayed that to Jamie. "Let me know what else you find, Jamie. Thanks." He put his cell back into his quilted jacket pocket, and thought that Vince DeGroot probably owned a cell phone. He took a deep breath, raising his eyebrows, and leaned in closer to Hannah.

"I'm guessing you tried calling your father's cell phone?"

"He never owned a cell phone. He's probably dead, isn't he?" For the first time, Hannah showed emotion, but Bobby wasn't affected. It didn't seem real. There were no tears in her eyes. He would like to have told her that missing people normally show up again at some point—that it's rarely a murder or suicide—but he wasn't in the consoling mood. He hoped she was getting upset enough that she would start answering his questions about the horses, but she clammed up again when he went back to how the horses ended up in her father's barn.

"Okay, then." Bobby pushed back his chair and stood. Hannah looked up at him. "I'm going to have to take you in to Newtown until we can get some answers from you. Get your coat, boots, whatever you need for a few hours." She looked at him in disbelief.

"I can't leave my mother here alone. Surely, you know that much," she hissed.

Bobby did know that, but he was hoping he could get her to talk by threatening a jail visit. When that didn't work, he decided he and Al could take off. Just as he knew Hannah couldn't leave her mother alone, he knew she wasn't going anywhere. He headed to the living room followed by Hannah. She pulled tissues from her pocket and bent down to wipe her mother's runny nose and drooling mouth.

"It's okay, Mom," she said. "Let's take a little nap, okay?"

"Don't leave the county, Hannah." Bobby instructed as he turned and walked out the door.

Sheriff Hanley and Al stood outside their cars in the DeGroots' yard and listened to the horses whinnying in the barn. The sound was pure and simple in the cold morning air. They stared at the house and then the barn. Hanley asked Al to notify Harvey Junior that the missing horses were found, and someone needed to come identify them.

"Tell him to bring any papers they have that would help ID them." He looked around at the run-down sheds and outbuildings. A corncrib with peeling white paint leaned sideways battered by winds. He felt he was going at the case backwards. Two men were missing. The horses were found on one of the men's farms. That man's daughter was hiding something and withholding information, he was sure of it. As soon as Al put his cell phone away and told him Harvey Junior was on his way, Bobby asked him what Mrs. DeGroot said while they were alone in the living room.

"I kept my word and didn't ask her any questions. Not sure it would have done any good if I had asked her anything. She never looked directly at me, but muttered the whole time. Most of it was incoherent, but she kept saying, "horse" or "horses" and "good horse." At one point, she became agitated and said she had to go see the horses, or clean the horses. I couldn't quite make it out. I told her we'd go see the horses later, and she calmed down, but kept muttering to herself. Once in awhile, she'd be still and just seem to drift off, but most of the time she seemed downright tormented." He paused thoughtfully. "Did Hannah tell you how eight stolen horses turned up in her barn?" Al pulled his gloves out of his pockets and put them on. "What is it today? In the teens? I thought it was supposed to warm up." He pulled his stocking cap down over his ears.

Bobby thought about Mrs. DeGroot's apparent obsession with horses.

"Al, we need to find out who Edith Edna DeGroot was before she married Vince, and we need to find out if the DeGroots owned horses previously. They sure have a lot of equipment and gear for horses, and some of it would cost a pretty penny, which the DeGroots don't appear to have."

"I'll get on it, Sheriff. I'm picking Kevin up at the Nook at seventeen hundred, but I'll have all afternoon to do some digging." Bobby chuckled inwardly at Al's military time reference, but knew Al was quickly becoming the best deputy he had.

Chapter 9

I made a quick dash out the front door to retrieve the morning newspapers. The *Des Moines Register* was right outside the door on the front porch, but the weekly Holland paper must have been buried in snow. I'd need to do some shoveling before heading to the Nook. If I was lucky, I could fire up my small snow blower that was on its last leg, get to the Nook by ten and be ready to head to Anamosa by the time Kevin showed up at one o'clock. I washed down a piece of toast with cranberry juice and counted it a serving of fruit. Quickly scanning the paper, the word "Monroe" caught my eye. Bobby. Yes, he'd be looking for those horses today, I thought. Would he be thinking of me? I read the short article. Most people wouldn't give it a second glance, but I read it over and over feeling a close connection to Bobby. A connection that might disappear if he moved to Vegas.

> **Monroe:** The Jasper County sheriff's office is investigating the apparent theft of eight horses near Monroe. Jasper County Sheriff Robert Hanley says the horses were stolen

sometime last week. Hanley says there is little evidence because of the recent heavy snowfall.

The next item that caught my eye was a huge hog manure spill into the North Raccoon River in western Iowa. Residents of Sac City would not have clean drinking water for days. That was one thing I didn't like about Iowa. Large hog confinement facilities and overuse of crop fertilizers were polluting our rivers and streams and lakes. I supposed that could be one good reason for moving to Las Vegas, but would a shortage of water be better than dirty water? Maybe I should make a list of pros and cons like Bobby suggested. I knew I'd made a mistake when I told him I couldn't think of any pros. He'd been hurt and asked if living with him wasn't a pro. Of course, I'd assured him, just not in Las Vegas.

The snow blower started with some encouragement, and it took only a few minutes to get the sidewalk cleared. The steps could wait. I took Archie with me, and we were helping our first customer by ten-fifteen. Noni had asked what I needed for the pastry counter, and I surveyed the small shelves of mostly leftover holiday cookies and candies. The Velveeta fudge had been a hit and was gone. I threw out the stale cookies and packaged up the candies to take to the homeless shelter. Then, I phoned Noni and told her to make something of her own choosing. She chose lemon bars and said she'd have them ready by the time I got home from Anamosa. Noni had been supplying the Book Nook with her home-baked pastries for six months. They were popular, and we both worked hard to make sure our pastries wouldn't compete with the Dutch bakerie's pastries. Besides, making Dutch letters was an art in itself—one neither Noni nor I had mastered.

I found the "Help Wanted" sign and was placing it in the front window when I noticed Bobby's toy train in the Christmas display. Once again, I felt a tug at my heart. How could I keep him here? Truth was I didn't know how, and I didn't know if I should try. He would do what he needed to do, I thought dismally. I needed to check the weather. Only light snow was forecast for the afternoon, so I was set for my drive to Anamosa to visit Killian in prison. I wasn't exactly looking forward to it, but I wanted to see for myself that Killian was okay. Normally, I would have called Bobby to tell him my plans, but there was no need. I knew he was busy, and I knew he had my number. I contemplated taking down the shop's Christmas tree, but the thought depressed me. The white lights and red berries looked festive and cheered me up when I plugged it in. It could wait until tomorrow or the next day.

A few customers wandered in and out, some standing outside looking at the front window before entering. I wasn't sure if they were looking at the display or the Help Wanted sign although no one expressed interest in the part-time job. Archie had fallen asleep on his rug in the children's section, and I was thinking of going next door to the deli for a sandwich when Kevin came through the front door with Stella in her carrier.

"Kevin, you're early."

He set the carrier down on the floor and opened the metal door. Stella leaped out and looked around stealthily like she was the star of a mouse-hunting documentary. We both laughed as she took off for the children's section and sat two inches from Archie's head waiting for him to wake up and notice her.

Kevin took off his coat and boots and explained why he was early, which had something to do with Al needing to drop him off and get back to the DeGroot farm.

"No problem, Kev. It's perfect. I'll just take off a little early, which will get me to Anamosa and back home before it gets dark, and, hopefully, before the big snow they say is coming. By the way, did you see the "Help Wanted" sign in the window?"

"Sure." He wrinkled his forehead and looked at me closely. "Like, are you letting me go?"

"No! Of course not! I just want you to have more time for your classes when vacation is over, and you need more time off for basketball practice and the games and everything else you're involved in. Twenty hours a week is too much for you right now, but I know you need the money, so I thought what I'd do is give you a raise. Not much, but it will help make up for the lack of hours, and it's just until basketball season is over. Does that sound all right?"

"Sure, but Al told you about the pot, right?"

"What?"

"The pot." He studied the floor. "Al found me smoking pot with some guys one night. He, like, thinks I need different friends. He thinks I'm not studying enough."

"Well, is that true? Are you studying enough?"

He laughed nervously. "No, I'm not, but my semester grades were okay. I didn't like flunk anything. It's been kind of hard. But, did he tell you about the pot, or not?"

"No, Kevin, he didn't mention any pot." I wondered why Al hadn't mentioned it, but then again, why would he? I'm not Kevin's parent or sponsor or anything really other than a caring employer. I appreciated Al keeping it confidential. "Kevin, Al wants what's best for you, and he wouldn't tell me or anyone about your smoking pot unless he felt it was a real problem. Did he talk to you about it?"

"Sure. I don't even smoke, and it wasn't a big deal to me." He shrugged his shoulders. "I just did it like to be one of the guys, you know?" I thought back to my teen years and laughed. Had I really put pumpkins in laundromat dryers, starting them up with quarters, and racing for cover down the street during a Halloween slumber party?

"Ah, yes, I do know." I gave him a quick hug letting him know the matter was settled as far as I was concerned. Then, I told him what to do if anyone came in interested in the part-time job, and I showed him where the job applications were. Soon, Archie and I were in the car headed north on our way to the state penitentiary.

As I entered the ramp to I-80, the car ahead of me hit the brakes in some slush. I skidded and almost rear-ended it. I gripped the steering wheel tightly until I'd driven a mile or two on mostly snow-cleared interstate. As I relaxed, I sped up to about fifty-five miles per hour, which seemed to be what everyone else was driving. I turned on the radio hoping to hear Christmas music, but instead they were playing pop songs. What the heck? They start playing Christmas music right after Halloween but they can't play it just one day after Christmas? I pulled off my fleece hat and threw it on the seat beside me, and successfully unzipped my down parka without unbuckling the seat belt. I was making good time and would be at the prison by one-thirty barring any kind of road closing or car accident. I let my mind wander, and wondered what Bobby was doing. I checked my cell phone to make sure it was on, and put it on the dash so I could hear it ring.

The drive to Anamosa was uneventful, but the further north I drove, I had to slow down considerably. I enjoyed watching the wintry landscapes change, but also had to keep an eye on the road for patches of ice. The drifted snow banks on the north side of the road reminded me of fluffy seven-minute frosting sculpted with a giant spatula, marred only by occasional snowmobile tracks. In places, the snow banks looked like rows of identical ocean waves peaking with a curlicue like children sometimes draw.

Tired of pop music, I changed to NPR. The bright sun on the glistening white snow was giving me a headache, so I popped my sun clips on my eyeglasses and lowered the windshield visor. I thought back to my last visit with Killian in October. I'd been shocked at his close-cropped hair and how much had turned gray. His mustache and heavy eyebrows were still coal black, however, and his wide-set eyes were still blue as a tropical sea. More wrinkles around his eyes and a thinner face made me wonder about the prison life he was now living. I'd vowed then to visit once a month, but November had been busy at the store and I'd wanted to see him before Christmas. I thought the day after Christmas would have to suffice. The prison didn't allow any gifts or food or even a Christmas card, and I felt the barren void in my hands, but not in my heart. I hoped my visit would be enough.

Killian had been convicted of second-degree murder for his part in the death of a local farmer, Doug Garrison, last May and was serving a fifty-year sentence at the state penitentiary. The real murderer was Garrison's wife, but Killian had wanted revenge on Garrison for years and "intended" to kill him. The result was that Killian knocked Garrison unconscious, but it was Mrs. Garrison who finished the job by hacking off her husband's leg with a chain saw and letting him bleed to death in the middle of the Neal Smith Wildlife Refuge. Bobby explained to me that the sentence is set under Iowa law for second-degree murder charges, and that Killian must serve seventy percent of the sentence before he is eligible for parole. My worry was that Killian would not survive that long in prison.

The terrain had turned hilly as I crossed the Wapsipinicon River. The drive from Holland to Anamosa would normally take an hour and a half, but today it took an extra hour due to patches of snow and ice on the roads. It made me wonder if I'd be driving home at dusk when deer tended to be lazily crossing roads. I hoped not. Weekday visits at the prison could last up to three hours, but I didn't think I'd stay that long. Killian probably wouldn't want me to stay that long, but I wasn't sure. I'd play it by ear. I'd studied the "Visiting Guideline" for the prison and knew I was only allowed fifteen dollars in the visiting room to use in the vending machines. I also knew they'd done a background check on me after Killian had filled out the inmate's Request for Visitor form.

I pulled off Highway 151 onto Anamosa's Main Street, then onto High Street and up the long hill to the prison. Bare oak trees of winter lined the street. I parked in front of what looked like a Gothic castle straight out of Jane Eyre. It was made of limestone from nearby quarries. There were turrets or parapets on top of the four-story building, and one large tower over the old main entrance in front. A wing jutted out from each side of the main building, all of which was covered with red tile roofing. It was strikingly beautiful and had been built by inmates in 1872. It housed over a thousand inmates and was on the National Register of Historic Places.

I parked in the street and put Archie on his leash. We walked a couple of blocks and headed back to the car. It was cold and windy on top of the hill, and he was happy to jump back into the warm car. I looked around at the children's park across the street, and the Grant Wood snow-covered hills behind the prison. The peaceful and quiet outdoors seemed at odds with the sounds of ordered confinement on the inside. I locked my car and headed to the main visitor entrance.

Upon entering the prison lobby, I was instructed to place my purse, cell phone, or any recording device in a locker and to obtain a token to operate the locker key from the lobby officer. I was not searched. I knew from prior visits that no cameras, no reading materials, no pets, and no games were allowed. A limit of twenty-five photos could be carried inside to show the inmate, but no Polaroid photos were allowed, and all photos must be taken back out of the institution with the visitor. If I needed medication while visiting, I would have to get an envelope from an officer and complete all information requested regarding the medication. When needed, the medication had to be taken in the presence of a staff member. No tobacco is allowed inside the building. None of this presented a problem for me. I was processed and ushered into the visiting area, where chairs were squared up to each table and were not to be moved without staff approval. I sat at an empty table and waited for Killian.

"Your friend, Sheriff Hanley, is a decent man, Mary Jo, even though he was convinced I killed Doug Garrison."

"I know, Killian. He acted like an *eejit* for awhile, but he also knew I didn't believe it, and he listened to me. He listened to you, too."

"How do ye know the meaning of *eejit*? Or do ye?"

"Moron?"

"Close enough." Killian laughed. I looked at my watch and then felt guilty. He wasn't even allowed to wear a watch. I looked up at him, but his gaze was focused on something behind me, or above me. "My sister used to call me *eejit* all the time."

I had never heard Killian mention his sister before or talk about anyone in his family except his daughter. I didn't interrupt him. He seemed to be remembering his past, and I thought maybe this was a good thing. Therapeutic even. Who else does a prisoner get to talk to? He leaned forward in his chair with both arms resting on the table. His face turned serious and was only inches from mine when he began to speak softly as if about to tell me a secret.

"She was murdered outside our house one night. I was only twelve, but I remember everything about that night."

I stared at Killian in wonder. His voice dropped an octave and was so soft I had to strain to hear him.

"I went to bed with me younger brothers, who were already asleep, when I heard voices downstairs. The voices got louder as I got out of bed. I snoock out to the landing." He looked up at me then as if to see how I was taking all this. I nodded to let him know he had my attention. Heck, I couldn't have ignored him if I'd wanted to.

"Six men in dark clothes were talking to me mam and sister. Da worked the night shift. He wasn't home. I later found out those men were IRA. This was in the eighties, when the clash between Protestants and Catholics was comin' to a head. There were riots every night, ye know, and children were forced to stay inside. Teenagers had no fun unless they snoock out. My sisters joked about what to wear to 'the riots.'"

He paused and smiled slightly as if remembering, and then took a deep breath. He continued to talk while I sat in the hard steel chair, mesmerized.

"Unfortunately for us, our house was across the street from the *garda* station. We were Catholic and sympathized with the

IRA, but I wasn't likin' them in our house in the middle of the night. Each man was dressed in black. Each held a gun. Me mam and sister were scared. The voices got louder and me younger brothers woke up."

Killian stopped then, ran his hand through his hair, and leaned back in his chair. His voice had cracked. He looked around him to see if anyone was listening. I waited in silence unaware of anyone else in the large room. It seemed hours before he started to talk again.

"When it was all over, our family was told the men were there to set up a sniper rifle in our house, but we weren't knowin' that then. When the *garda* changed shifts, these men planned to shoot as many *garda* as they could. What they didn't know was me sister, Margaret Ann, had a crush on Garda Ned Clapham. She was not about to let him get shot."

Killian sat back in his chair, looking at me, but seeing someone or something else.

"In the middle of the night, she snoock out of our house to warn the *garda*. The sniper shot her in the back. She was halfway across the street. The two *garda* who ran out in the street to help her were shot down, too."

He looked at me then with tearless eyes. I had the feeling he'd already shed many a tear and none were left.

"End of story. That's the way it was in Northern Ireland in the eighties." There wasn't a trace of emotion in his voice.

I was speechless. The visiting room seemed unusually quiet. A prisoner and his visitor sitting next to us had stopped talking and were listening to Killian instead. Of course, I'd known about Northern Ireland's history and the "trouble" between the Protestants and Catholics. I knew their cemeteries were filled with young people who had been killed in riots. I remembered with pride when President Bill Clinton went over in the nineties and helped broker the peace treaty that ended those riots. It had seemed so far away from my world. Now, even my bones seemed to feel the violence. I mentally tried to compare my childhood to that of Killian's, but there was no comparison to be made. Ireland was a war-torn country seeking freedom from British rule. Protestants and Catholics fought and killed each other. Catholic churches were burned. Children were harassed on their way to school. Revolutionaries were imprisoned for life.

"Killian, I'm so sorry." I grabbed one of his hands in mine being grateful there was no partition between us like you see on TV shows. He looked at me intensely.

"Mary Jo, ye've been a good friend these past six years." I wanted to argue that point, because I was feeling guilty that I'd never worked very hard to be Killian's friend. I'd been his employee at the Book Nook, and I'd supported him throughout his trial, but good friends would have done more. But that was history. Right now, I knew I'd do anything I could for Killian. If he asked me to bake him a cake with a knife hidden inside, I would do that. I smiled at the thought.

"Ye have a nice smile, lass. I'm going to miss it." My heart thunked. *What was he talking about now?*

"When I get out of here, I'll be goin' back home."

"Home?" I was confused. I didn't want to hear what might be coming next.

"Ireland. Me home." He looked at me patiently. "I don't know when, or how, but that is what I'm plannin' to do." I stared at him not knowing which question to ask first.

"When you are released from here, you want to go back to Ireland?" I thought back to my marriage counseling period. *Repeat their question to clarify, which gives you more time to respond*, I remembered the counselor telling me. Now, it was Killian's turn to smile.

"Aye. Ye heard me correctly. I plan to go back to Ireland when I'm released. Of course, I'll have to talk to me barrister about it, and work out arrangements, but I've been told t'will be possible. The reason I'm tellin' ye now this far in advance is I'm wantin' to deed the Nook to ye. I want ye to have me shop, Mary Jo. No one else."

A buzzer went off and the door opened. I was ushered out into the hall by an armed guard. I retrieved my personal things from the tray slid to me under the wire partition, and walked back to my car without a backward glance. I could see Archie awake and sitting in the front passenger seat. I let him out and walked him down the hill and back up the other side. He marked his territory on several limestone light posts and sniffed under every shrub and bush we passed.

"Good dog, Arch." I praised while pulling a milk biscuit out of my coat pocket before letting him back in the car. He chewed in silence. I looked around at the white, snow-covered hills. The sky was darkening and snowflakes fell slowly. I felt reluctant to leave. I couldn't imagine what Killian's life was like behind bars every day. I held the back door open for Arch and he bounded inside.

Heading out of town, I didn't see one person on the sidewalks. Some towns were hit harder by the economy than others, and I was glad Holland was faring better than most. I turned up the radio.

"KNIK's latest weather update! Snow continues to fall with a low pressure system moving in from Colorado. Temperatures will fall into the single digits overnight and winds will pick up. Tomorrow we're looking at accumulations of six to eight more inches, making this the snowiest December since 1988. So, get out and get those Christmas gifts returned or exchanged today, because tomorrow you may be stuck indoors."

All I could think of was Killian's news, which he had saved for last. The judge had accepted a motion for a new trial. Killian's defense attorney had argued that there was no evidence at trial that Killian could have predicted Garrison would be mutilated and killed by his wife after Killian punched him. I needed to ask Bobby about that. Was it possible that Killian could be found not guilty and released?

Chapter 10

Bobby watched as Al made a three-point turn in his green Jeep Rubicon and headed out DeGroots' snow-covered lane. Then, he tapped in headquarters' phone number and was relieved when Jamie answered. She never asked unnecessary questions. What he needed from her now was a deputy bearing an arrest warrant for Hannah DeGroot, and someone from the Department of Human Services to stay with Hannah's mother indefinitely. He saw an opportunity to take Hannah DeGroot to jail and question her before indecision paralyzed him. He knew if he waited, she would have an edge, but he also knew they could not leave her mother alone in the house. Hopefully, by arresting Hannah before noon, she could still get before a judge on a bail motion that afternoon, and be back home by evening to take care of her mother. Maybe bail wasn't even necessary for a horse-rustling case.

So, he sat in DeGroots' lane waiting for Harvey Junior to come identify the horses as his, and a deputy with an arrest warrant for Hannah. Had he ever heard of a horse rustling case in

Iowa? He wasn't sure. He didn't want Hannah or her mother to suffer needlessly. He just wanted the truth.

He got into his Pathfinder and started the engine to keep warm. He thought briefly of calling Mary Jo to see what she was up to. He couldn't remember if she was working at the Nook all day, and then realized it was the first time in ages he didn't know her plans. Scott and Tennille's visit, and a surprise Christmas Eve baby, left little time for Mary Jo. If he felt guilty, it didn't last long. A dirty, black Dodge Ram pickup pulling a large horse trailer drove slowly into the farmyard and stopped beside Bobby's car. Bobby got out and greeted Harvey Junior as he jumped down from the truck.

"I have bills of sale for each of the eight horses belonging to my dad." Harvey said as he handed the sheriff a torn and tattered manila folder bulging with a mess of papers. Bobby looked up into the cab of the pickup and saw two teenage girls staring back at him. "The girls can help me load the horses, Sheriff. I don't want to be here any longer than I have to. You going to arrest these people for stealing our horses?" he asked matter-of-factly. Bobby explained that he was waiting for an arrest warrant for Hannah DeGroot.

"Mrs. DeGroot isn't well and can't be left alone, so I've asked for someone from DHS to come sit with her. I can help with the horses 'til they get here with the warrant. They're in that shed over there," Bobby pointed to the rundown building farthest from the house.

Harvey motioned for his girls to follow, and they slid out of the truck's cab.

"These two are my daughters, Ellie and Georgia," Junior said. Bobby saw for the first time they were identical twins. They wore gold Carhartt jackets frayed at the cuffs with hooded sweatshirts underneath for warmth. Their well-worn black rubber boots showed tears. They seemed excited to see the horses and raced ahead of their father and the sheriff. When they got to the shed, they stopped and, stamping their feet to keep warm or from excitement, waited for the men to open the sliding door.

"Fudgie, Toad," they screamed as they ran up to the horses. "Dad, look at Puff with the ribbons in her mane." The girls went in different directions checking out each horse, and hugging their necks, and kissing their faces. Bobby felt relief. There was no question whose horses these were although he intended to study each bill of sale back at his office.

A car horn honked and Bobby left the barn to see if it was a deputy with the arrest warrant. When he saw a woman carrying a briefcase exit the passenger side of a county sheriff's car, he was doubly relieved. The arrest warrant *and* the DHS worker to stay with Edith Edna. How did Jamie manage that, he wondered. It meant he could arrest Hannah immediately and remove her from the premises before the Johnsons started loading up the horses. He introduced himself to the DHS worker and explained the circumstances to her. Then, they headed up the steps to the house.

Bobby anticipated a scene when arresting Hannah, but she invited him and the social worker inside. He explained that he was there to arrest her and introduced the woman from DHS. Hannah nodded silently. She did start to cry when she showed the DHS employee to the bedroom where her mother was sleeping. They watched as Hannah pulled a crocheted afghan up over her mother.

"She'll want a cup of tea and some cookies when she wakes up. I set everything out on the kitchen table," she choked back tears. She went to the front closet and pulled out her coat and boots. "Do I need to bring anything? Will I be in jail all night?" she asked Bobby.

He explained to her how he hoped the afternoon would go, and told her they just wanted the truth about how the Johnson horses ended up in her barn. The sooner she told him the truth, the sooner she could be out of jail on bail. She slipped off her shoes and pulled on her boots.

"Who do you think is going to bail me out, Sheriff?"

"Let's cross that bridge when we come to it. Here," he helped her on with her coat, and then unclipped the handcuffs from his utility belt. She didn't resist when he locked the handcuffs over her wrists, but looked up at him incredulously.

"Sorry. Regulations." He took her arm and led her out the front door and down the steps. Johnson had backed the horse trailer as close to the shed as possible. Hannah stopped in her tracks and watched as one of the twins led a horse through the open door of the trailer. Bobby waited a few seconds and then nudged her toward his car.

Once in the interrogation room with mugs of hot tea in front of them, Bobby turned on a recording device and asked Hannah if she was willing to speak to him about her involvement in the theft of eight horses. He showed her the waiver form and asked her to sign and date it if she was willing to proceed with the interrogation. If, at that point, she requested the presence of a lawyer there would be no interrogation. She read the waiver and signed it. Bobby could only guess why she didn't ask for an attorney. He hoped it meant she was willing to tell him everything she knew

The interrogation did not go well. It did not go *anywhere* in fact. Somewhere between her house and the jail in Newtown, Hannah became belligerent. She had kicked the back of his seat several times and swore at him when he rounded a curve too fast throwing her a little off balance. Now, she answered all the unimportant questions, but when it came to the horses, she refused to speak. She wouldn't even look him in the eye. The threat of being kept in a cell all night did not seem to affect her. The suggestion that she could be back home with her mother soon did not move her to talk.

"Have you ever been processed after an arrest, Hannah?" Bobby asked changing tack. She had been slumped down into her chair with fatigue, but sat up straight.

"No. I don't even know what that means." She began nervously chewing her bottom lip but stopped when she tasted blood. Bobby leaned across the table and looked her in the eye.

"It means you are photographed, fingerprinted, stripped of your clothes, given a body search with a flashlight and a rubber glove, and issued an orange jumpsuit." He paused so what he'd described could sink in. "I would prefer that you tell me what you know about the horses, and I'll drive you home myself. Or, do you want to sit in jail for weeks and eventually go to trial? Because finding the missing horses in your barn is pretty much all the evidence we need to prosecute you." He felt a trickle of perspiration under his heavy department-issued sweater, but held his gaze on her eyes. She blinked several times and lowered her head. Bobby studied her thoughtfully.

"I'd like to hear your version of what happened, Hannah."

"I don't have a version, Sheriff. I think I need a lawyer," she said tiredly.

Chapter 11

Nearing the exit to Holland on my way home from Anamosa, I slowed down. Snow was still falling, not heavily, but steadily in large soft flakes. Several Canada geese sat in the ditch along the road and stared at me as I maneuvered the curve. More geese landed near them as I picked up speed. Archie slept peacefully in the back seat. My mind was full of Killian's news, but I began to wonder why I hadn't heard from Bobby all day. It was unusual not to check in with each other at least once a day, so I vowed I'd call him as soon as I got home. First, I wanted to stop at the Nook to see if Kevin needed help closing up. The car clock said it was five-fifteen p.m. which meant Kevin might still be there.

I parked in front of the Nook and saw Kevin inside at the cash register. He had already hung the "Closed" sign on the door, but the shop looked bright and cheerful through the plate glass window. All the lights were on and the Christmas tree in the corner sparkled with white fairy lights. Snowflakes fell slowly from the darkening sky. It hit me then that I might someday be the owner of this shop I'd learned to love.

"Mrs. McGee, Archie." Kevin mumbled with a smile as he looked up from his work. Several dead leaves blew in through the door with us. Archie bounded up to Kevin like he was his long lost friend, and I could tell Kevin was happy to see us. After petting and scratching Archie's ears, Kevin began to tell me about the afternoon's transactions that had been few. He had a question about a book return, and I was happy he did it correctly without my help.

"I'm glad there was only one. I wasn't sure. Somebody did come in and apply for the part-time job."

"No! Who?" I was surprised and could hardly wait to find out while Kevin searched the counter for the application.

"A Lola VandeKamp," he said as he handed me the application smiling. My heart sank.

"Lola VandeKamp?" I looked at the paper in my hands and began to read what she'd filled out.

"I sprinkled some salt on the sidewalk. She told me she like slipped on some ice out front. I shoveled some snow and chopped up a layer of ice. I'll go out and pick up those dead leaves, too," he said as he headed for his Central College jacket by the door.

"Don't bother, Kevin. The wind will take them, or they'll be buried in snow soon anyway." I looked to the bottom of the page to see who Lola had put down for her three references. Her cousin, Al Lawson, who happened to be my daughter's fiancé, was listed first. Then, Robert Hanley, Sheriff of Jasper County, and, third was George VandeKamp, her ex-husband. No former employers were listed, and I tried to remember if I had ever known Lola to be employed. Noni would know. I wished I had been here when Lola came in. Last June, she'd flirted with Bobby and nearly ruined the blossoming relationship between Bobby and me.

"I told her you'd get in touch with her. I like let it slip that no one else had applied. Sorry." He looked sheepish.

"No problem, Kevin. I know Lola, sort of. I'll wait a day or two, see if anyone else applies, and call her," shrugging my shoulders in a no-big-deal attitude. "Let's lock up and I'll run you home."

I couldn't wait to get home and call Bobby. Maybe he'd left a message on my home phone. I was excited to tell him about Killian getting a new trial and possibly being released. I was still in disbelief that Killian wanted to give me ownership of the Book Nook. Give me ownership? Admittedly, the thought thrilled me. My mind wandered to changes I would like to make in the shop, including changing the name. I'd always thought Book Nook was a ho-hum name. I was trying out some Dutch names aloud when my house came into view. I pulled into the driveway and let Archie out of the car. We spotted Noni sweeping snow off their front steps, and Archie bounded over to greet her. By the time I slogged through the drifts to their front steps, Archie was rolling around in the snow like a dog who had been cooped up in a car all afternoon.

"Hey, stranger," Noni greeted me. She looked like an ad for vintage clothing with her brown plaid wool coat, fur-trimmed zipper boots and a perky green tam balanced jauntily on her Dutchboy haircut.

"Hey, yourself," I huffed and puffed as I stomped my boots on the sidewalk. "Brrr. Getting colder."

"Come on in. Joe's getting groceries and I've got a pot of soup simmering." She motioned me to follow her in.

"Stay, Archie." I followed Noni inside but explained I was anxious to get home and phone Bobby. She wanted to know how the new baby was, and I was ashamed I couldn't tell her. I really should have called Bobby earlier. It also dawned on me that I hadn't even thought about a baby gift for Noelle. Maybe some baby books from the Nook? Most new moms appreciated books, I thought.

"Earth to Mary Jo." Noni startled me. "Where were you just now?" She was laughing, so I explained what I'd been thinking.

"Books for a new baby are always welcome, but then you and I were teachers. Maybe not everyone appreciates books the way you and I do." She took the lid off a steaming pot and stirred the soup. It smelled delicious. "Sure you can't stay? It's vegetable beef," trying to tempt me.

"No. Really. I have to talk to Bobby, but before I go I want to tell you about my visit with Killian." Noni had forgotten I was going to Anamosa today but wanted to hear all about it. I'd just gotten to the part about Killian wanting me to be the owner of his shop when Joe came through the back door carrying two bags of groceries in each hand. Out of breath, he plopped them down on the counter while Noni scolded him for tracking in wet snow on her clean kitchen floor. As much as I loved this domestic scene between Noni and Joe, I was anxious to get home.

"Hey, I'll let you two get on with your dinner. Oh, by the way Noni, Lola VandeKamp applied for a part-time job at the Nook today. Do you happen to know if she's ever worked anywhere else? She listed Bobby, Al and her ex-husband as her only references, which is kind of odd. Do you know if she's got any employment history?"

Noni was surprised Lola applied to work at the Nook with me and couldn't remember ever seeing her employed anywhere. She assured me she'd let me know if she thought of something. I left and found Archie waiting for me on the front porch.

As soon as I got out of my coat and boots, I checked my phone for messages. None. I checked my watch and wondered what Bobby might be doing. I poured myself a glass of wine and punched in his cell phone number. By the time he answered, I was curled up in a corner of the sofa with my feet tucked under me for warmth.

"Is it too late to invite you to dinner, Bobby?" I asked.

"I'm afraid so, Red. I'm on my way to the hospital and thought I'd just grab a bite there with Scott."

"Oh." I swallowed my disappointment. "How are they all doing? I mean is the baby still okay? Will Tennille be discharged soon?"

"Tennille was discharged this morning but stayed all day to nurse Noelle. Hey, why don't you come over to the hospital and we could all eat together? The cafeteria isn't too bad."

I didn't see that coming, but I should have. Of course, Bobby would want to spend his evenings with his son and his new family. However, I did not want to go out again. I was tired and it was snowing. I just wanted to stay home with Archie. Maybe start a fire in the fireplace and eat leftovers. I also wanted to spend time with Bobby, but not in a hospital cafeteria with Scott along. Do hospital cafeterias now serve beer, I thought maliciously. I shivered and stood to check the thermostat.

"Bobby, I'm really beat. I don't think I can come over. I was gone all day. I drove to Anamosa to visit Killian. I'd like to talk to you some time about it but not tonight and not at the hospital. Some time when we can be alone." I heard my stomach rumble.

"Okay, sure. I'd like that. It's been quite a day for me, too. Did Al tell you we found the missing horses?"

Al hadn't told me. I hadn't talked to Al when he dropped Kevin off at the Nook. Bobby proceeded to tell me about finding the horses at some DeGroot farm near Monroe—near the farm the horses were missing from which struck me as odd.

"It is odd, Red. I had to arrest the young DeGroot woman. Her mother has Alzheimer's and her father isn't around, or at least that's what Hannah, the daughter, told me. It's all odd, and I think there is a connection between the missing horses and the missing Harvey Johnson."

"Hmmm," I yawned. "Has there never been any sign or clue as to where he might be?"

"Nope, but we might get something out of Hannah DeGroot. Anyway, I'm pulling into the hospital now. Would you like me to call you when I get home tonight?"

"Sure. I'll be here. I might go to bed early though."

"I'll call by nine."

We said our good-byes and I settled in for my evening of TV and leftovers. As I heated my dinner in the microwave, I realized Bobby hadn't even asked me about my trip to Anamosa.

When the phone rang at ten p.m., it startled me. I'd evidently fallen asleep on the sofa watching *Castle,* which was too bad because Beckett and Castle were just figuring out who the murderer was when I must have drifted off. Bobby sounded as tired as I felt.

"Sorry for not calling earlier, Mary Jo. Scott and Tennille needed a ride here, and I hung around a little helping them get the baby settled in for the night. I'm really excited about something though and want to talk to you about it."

"Sure. I'm all ears." I sat up and turned off the TV with the remote.

Bobby proceeded to tell me about Scott's idea of Bobby flying out to Las Vegas with them to "check things out" and see how he'd like it. Of course, I was invited, too.

"Would you like that, Red? A few days' vacation in Vegas with me?"

"Bobby. I don't know." I stalled. I didn't want to go to Las Vegas to "check things out." Why would I? I didn't want to move there and I couldn't understand why Bobby was considering moving there. I didn't even believe he was serious about it. It seemed preposterous, but what could I say?

"Bobby, are you sure you want to move to Las Vegas? It just seems so strange to me."

"Strange, Mary Jo? You think it's strange for someone to want to live near his son and granddaughter?"

"No, that's not what I meant," I said grudgingly. I was too tired to have this conversation. "It just seems so sudden."

"Mary Jo. Listen to me. When Scott suggested I move to Las Vegas with him and Tennille, I was surprised and thought 'no way.' But, I was also flattered. My son wants to be near me. My son wants a relationship with me. My son, who'd always kept me at arm's length now wants me to live close to him. I have to admit, I've felt guilty about never having enough time to spend with him while he was growing up. Law enforcement caused crazy hours, and I missed most of his Little League games, you know.

"But, Bobby," I interrupted.

"No, hear me out, Mary Jo. Just hear me out, will you?"

"Sorry, Bobby. Go on. I'm listening."

"Okay, then. Here's the thing. Scott dropped out of Scouts because I was never there to help like the other dads. Plus, he and Tennille have just had the most beautiful baby girl and I loved her at first sight. When I hold her in my arms, I know I want to watch her grow on a daily basis. I don't want to be one of those grandparents who get the annual school photo in their mailbox once a year or the occasional visit to Iowa. Why can't you understand that?"

"I do, Bobby. I do. I just, I just know I don't want to move away from here. I'm sorry, but I just can't even think about it," I paused. "I'm really tired, Bobby. Can we talk about it tomorrow night?"

"Sure. Sure. You sound like you need some sleep. I know I do. I'll call tomorrow night," and with that, he hung up. No sweet *good-bye* or *sleep tight* or pet names. I let Archie out to do his duty and put my dirty dishes in the dishwasher.

Then, I stepped out on the back porch and listened to the total silence of snow falling. Tears stung my eyes. I missed Bobby horribly, and it hit me like a lightning bolt that I might be losing him forever. Archie came lumbering up to me covered in snow and nudged my leg with his snowy snout.

We headed inside and got ready for bed. I opened the shade to watch the snow falling. Little icy snow pebbles gathered in the corners of the window. New Year's Eve was four days away, and this was to be Bobby's and my first New Year's Eve together. Now, it sounded like he might be spending it in Las Vegas. I crawled into bed and wished Bobby was there making plans with me. My last thought before falling asleep was how the copper-colored hairs on Bobby's forearms looked in sunlight.

Chapter 12

"Are you serious?"

Al slid the folder across the desk to Bobby.

"As serious as I can be." Al chuckled. "Edith Edna DeGroot knows her way around horses. Just look at that photo."

Bobby had already opened the folder and was leafing through the papers. He looked up at Al who was still standing there in his department-issued winter jacket and uniform, his stocking cap stuffed in his front pocket.

Excited, Al began to recite a few of the highlights for Bobby. "She was Edith Edna Severino, daughter of Tarzan Severino, who came to the United States from Europe in the 1940s. They were an old French circus family with Italian roots. Edith Edna was an aerialist and equestrienne. Look, she's hanging under the horse while it's galloping around the ring. There's another photo of her somersaulting from the saddle to the ground. It really looks like her although she's changed. But, look at her face. That's her all right."

"I think you're right, Al, but what the … what does it mean? Edith Edna DeGroot was a circus performer who performed with horses when she was what? A teenager? Did you read all this, Al?"

"That's a Roger. Couldn't stop reading. It's fascinating stuff. I've never been to a circus and sure as heck never saw anything like that." He nodded toward the photos. "She performed from the time she was a child until she was in her thirties. I'm guessing that's about the time she met DeGroot and got married. Maybe got pregnant. I can't see anybody doing those tricks if they were pregnant."

"Right." Bobby agreed, but was already thinking ahead to the ramifications this new information had on the case. "Edith Edna DeGroot was Edith Edna Severino and traveled with a circus as a trick rider on horses most of her young life. This says a horse can get up a good gallop in a forty-two-foot ring but can't go much faster." He looked closer at the photos and used his pencil to circle a few words. There was one photo of her holding a pistol in each hand while riding a horse, reminding him of Annie Oakley photos. He'd have to remember that Edith Edna DeGroot was at least familiar with firearms and possibly a sharp shooter. "Looks dangerous to me." He looked up at Al. "These articles you found sound like Edith Edna DeGroot is a horse lover. The horses were found in DeGroots' barn. Hannah won't answer questions. Edith Edna has Alzheimer's. The horses are docile and Hannah is young and strong enough to load them into a horse trailer and unload them at their farm. But, why? Why would Hannah DeGroot steal her neighbor's horses?" Bobby stood up and began to pace. "It sounds like her mother grew up around horses her whole life. Al, didn't you tell me Edith Edna repeatedly said something about horses the day we were at their farm, but you couldn't make sense out of it?"

Al rubbed his hand over his shaved head and sat down in the chair by Bobby's desk. He would love to have had a theory, but all his thoughts seemed ludicrous—they were going to start up a circus in Holland, they just wanted to go horseback riding, they wanted to save on gas or they were going to try to sell them for profit. Only the last seemed to be a possibility.

"Yes, sir, she did, but I didn't get much out of it other than the word horses. She seemed worried about the horses. Do you think they stole those horses to sell?"

"Possibly, but who would they sell them to? Nobody around here. Everybody knows the Johnson horses went missing, and they'd be on the lookout for them." He tapped his teeth with his pencil. He knew Hannah had been released by dinnertime last night having been perceived as no threat.

"She might think she could haul them out to Montana and sell them, but since she can't leave her mother alone, she wouldn't just take off now." He hesitated and looked at Al. "We need to go back out there and question Hannah again." He gulped the last of his lukewarm tea and picked up the folder with the circus articles and photos. "Had any breakfast yet?"

"No, sir. Had to get Kevin to basketball practice by seven. I figured Jamie might still have some Dutch letters in the fridge."

Bobby laughed. He hadn't taken the time to make breakfast either. He hadn't really felt like eating and thought he'd phone Mary Jo as soon as he got to work, but then Al was waiting for him with this new information. He promised himself he'd call her when they finished at the DeGroot farm.

"Sure. She's got some chocolate fudge in there, too, but it's past prime. Let's grab a bite at McDonald's on the way out of town."

Chapter 13

Waking up feeling lethargic and depressed, I rolled over onto my side and pulled the covers up to my ears. I closed my eyes. I didn't hear Archie but knew he'd be waking up soon, too. Maybe he was in the kitchen already cleaning up any spilled nibbles around his dog dish.

The wind had died down and sunlight was peeking in around the window shade. This would be a good day to go snowshoeing, I thought. Not wanting to waste a beautiful morning feeling sorry for myself, I started making a to-do list in my head and soon joined Archie in the kitchen. First, I decided to unwrap my gift from Bobby. Might as well see what kind of suitcase he thought I might like. I ripped through the taped Christmas paper hurriedly. It was beautiful—brown and tan tapestry-looking, and it had wheels. When I opened it, I was surprised to find a smaller wrapped gift inside. I tore off the paper not knowing what could be inside. Not sure if I was pleased to find a new cell phone or not, I looked closer and discovered it was an Apple iPhone.

"Hmmm," and a red cover for it. I placed it back in the suitcase and decided to get salt on the front sidewalk. I knew there was a dangerous layer of ice underneath the new snow, and it wouldn't take long to tackle that chore. Getting that phone up and running could wait. I also knew Bobby was investigating the missing horses, and I had to admit I was a little curious as to who and why someone would kidnap their neighbor's horses. The name was DeGroot, and they lived outside of Monroe off the county road east of town. Maybe, I'd just take a swing by there between snowshoeing at the refuge and going to work at the Nook. This would be the perfect morning for snowshoeing on the trail. Soon, I was pulling on my long underwear. I can't say I was super excited, but it was better than sitting still and better than taking down my Christmas tree. I knew Bobby would call eventually, and I didn't want him to think I was moping around with nothing better to do than think of reasons why he shouldn't move to Las Vegas with Scott. It was true I didn't like Scott very much. I didn't like his drinking. I didn't like his boasting or his expensive cowboy boots or his lascivious glare at Pippi the other night. It was Pippi who said Scott seems to kill the spirit of any room he enters. That did seem true, but, he was Bobby's son, and I was determined not to be critical. Surely, Bobby saw Scott's faults. Didn't he, I wondered.

The prairie was covered in deep snow and sunlight shattered everything. I squinted at the brightness until my eyes adjusted. The refuge's visitor center has snowshoes in adult and children's sizes available for checkout. They're free and just need to be returned by the end of the day. I found a pair and carried them outside to put on. Feeling like a child with a new present, I headed up the hill on the trail. The earthy smell and frigid air reminded me of growing up on a farm and sledding with friends on nearby hills. I was all alone on the prairie trail having left Archie at home, but I felt safe. The land might be wild and open, but nature and various species of animals and birds thrive here. Nature is beautiful, and I wondered what kind of wildlife refuges Nevada has. Some people say the desert is beautiful. It wouldn't hurt to check into it, I thought.

After a mile or so, I veered off the trail. With as much snow as we had, this was not a problem. Less snow, and I'd be getting hung up on ground-nesting ant mounds. The mounds were humongous—for ants. But, the good thing is the ants aerated the soil better than earthworms which made the soil perfect for prairie plant growth. I stopped walking. The only sounds were bird calls. One may have been an evening grosbeak, which I knew had come south from Minnesota due to the drought up there. No rain, no seeds. More likely they were nuthatches or woodpeckers. I looked around and not seeing any birds, started walking again. Walking and walking in the pristine snow like good King Wenceslas.

Now, there wasn't a sound except for my steps in the snow as I trudged along burning off some of the calories I'd consumed over Christmas, or so I hoped. I stopped to catch my breath. Why was I pushing my body so hard? Sure, I loved snowshoeing but turning sixty last May made me feel, what? Old? Useless? I didn't like that my knees were hurting, not to mention my hips aching. I started up again in earnest. Ten more minutes, then I'd head back.

I came to a stand of black locust trees and could see where the rangers had tried to cull them. An invasive species, the black locust outcompetes many native, slower growing trees. They spread quickly because of their ability to resprout from the root system in a different location from the parent tree. This reminded me of Bobby and Scott again and saddened me. I wondered why Scott would all of a sudden want Bobby in his life. It hadn't occurred to me before that Scott was possibly not being totally honest with Bobby. Maybe Scott had money concerns? That could surely be reason to make up with daddy after fifteen years of ignoring his father, his roots, and his friends in Iowa. However, it wasn't my place to inquire or even to care. I considered myself a strong woman, not a woman who would compete for a man's affection, and certainly not one who would compete against the love of a man for his own child. Now remembering how excluded I felt when I saw Bobby and Scott sharing a laugh together, I had to ask myself if I was being totally honest about my feelings. I looked around me to see if any winter-thick, shaggy-coated buffalo could be spotted, and not seeing any, I decided to turn back to the visitor's center. I felt spiritually renewed as I pulled out of the parking lot, but, my knees definitely weren't feelin' the luv.

The weatherman on the car radio warned of low visibility 'til noon on Saturday. Seems a low pressure system was above us, and one was below us, with snow totals continuing to rack up before it moves out to the east. A high of twenty-nine degrees tomorrow. Yay, I thought. Almost warm enough to run the Honda through de Autowasplaats and get the street salt off.

Next stop would be the DeGroot farm. Well, not that I was planning on actually paying them a visit. I was just curious as to where they lived and what kind of people would steal their neighbor's horses?

I arrived in Monroe a little after nine-thirty. It was now partially cloudy and I took off my sunglasses at the stop sign. Bobby and Al had talked of the county road, so I turned east on Washington Street that soon turned into a gravel road. It was very hilly and my tires skidded on the steep upgrades. Darn. I did not want to get stuck and have to call someone to pull me out of a ditch. I hadn't realized there was this kind of hilly area near Holland. A flock of sheep stared at me as I rounded a corner. Fields were terraced and contoured around the hills, and except for an old cemetery with a few pine trees, there was not a lot to see. That is, unless you were looking for wildlife. I spotted two white-headed eagles in a large oak, and a few deer in a field. Then, I came to a lane with a small farmyard at the end. It had to be the DeGroots' because Al had said the small ranch-style house was mint green. Although faded, this was definitely a mint green house. A white propane gas tank covered in rust sat in the front yard. A late-model white Land Rover with Montana license plates sat next to the house. Not sure why, but I pulled off the road and stopped. I turned off the engine and got out.

I listened to the wind that had picked up and was blowing snow into drifts. I shivered in spite of still being overheated from snowshoeing. Something nagged at me. I heard the rustle of dry corn leaves. The lisping of dry corn stalks. Something wasn't right. Then, it hit me. The corn hadn't been picked. The corn in this field had not been picked before the snows came, which was very strange; although with Mr. DeGroot missing, and Edith Edna DeGroot having Alzheimer's, who did I think would pick twenty acres of corn? Neighbors, that's who. Surely neighbors would have volunteered to pick DeGroots' corn. A snow-covered anhydrous ammonia tank hibernated in the field. The soil lay fallow under the sea of snow and pale cornstalks. I felt a sense of apprehension. What else could be under that snow? I stood and stared another minute or two, and then got back into my car. I'd call Bobby and ask him if he noticed the corn hadn't been picked. My mind raced. Why wasn't it picked? Why didn't any neighbors offer to pick it for the DeGroot women? Maybe no one liked the DeGroots. That wouldn't matter. Neighbors help neighbors in need. There was a reason why that corn had never been picked, and I wanted to know why.

I turned around and headed back to Holland. With any luck, I'd be turning the "Open" sign around in the door of the Nook by ten o'clock. I'd see if anyone besides Lola VandeKamp had applied for the part-time job, and then I'd phone Bobby to tell him about the unpicked cornfield.

As it turned out, I didn't have to phone Bobby. I met him and Al turning into DeGroots' lane while I was just coming to a stop before turning onto the road. Bobby stopped as he pulled up beside me and rolled down his window. I did the same. He was grinning which was a good sign. I figured he'd be upset at me for snooping into his business about the missing horse case.

"Are you lost, Mary Jo?"

There was no way I could figure out any reason for being out here in the country when I should be heading to the Nook in town. Lord, he was handsome in a rugged sort of way. Yellow hair turning gray and huskie blue eyes that were now drilling into mine. I took a deep breath.

"Hi, Al," I waved my mittened hand. He gave me the two-finger salute grinning like Bobby. "Bobby, I'm on my way to work, really, but it's a good thing I took a detour because I noticed something." I looked back toward the farm. "Bobby, no one picked the corn in that one field back there. Does that belong to the DeGroots? Why wouldn't anyone offer to help them pick it knowing the man left the women all alone?" I looked at my watch like I was in a hurry—which I now was.

"That the best you can do, Red?" Bobby asked with a grin.

"Bobby, admit it. No one leaves their corn unpicked without a good reason, and even if they have a good reason like a farmer being sick or dead or whatever, the neighbors pick it for him. The more I think about it, the odder it seems. And, one other thing that occurred to me," my voice picked up speed and volume as I thought about that cornfield, "that unpicked cornfield back in July when DeGroot went missing would have been the perfect place to hide a dead body. The cornstalks being six foot high and all. Have you thought about that? Can you ask those women why none of the neighbors bothered to pick their corn?" I took a deep breath. "I've really got to be going now. I just think it's something to look into. That's all."

Bobby stared at me no longer grinning.

"I won't keep you then." He made no effort to roll up his window and drive away. He just kept staring at me. "The baby is being discharged this afternoon, Mary Jo. Scott and Tennille will be leaving for Las Vegas tomorrow."

"Oh." I wanted to ask a million questions, but nothing came out.

"They have a flight out in the morning, and I have a ticket, too."

"Oh." My heart was fluttering. My mind wasn't working properly, but I managed to ask, "When are you coming back?" My eyes started to fill with tears, and I quickly put on my sunglasses.

"I don't know. I won't stay long. I just want to help them get settled." He looked across the seat at Al who was looking out his window away from us. "We need to get going. I'll call you later," and off they went toward the DeGroot farm.

I automatically looked both ways before pulling out, although if a speeding truck T-boned me, I wouldn't have felt anything. I was numb. If Bobby flew to Las Vegas with Scott and Tennille tomorrow with little Noelle, that would mean he'd probably still be out there on New Year's Eve. I'd be alone on New Year's Eve. I've been there before and knew I'd survive, but I had been so excited to think of spending it with Bobby. Not one to go in for loud bars and the forced gaiety of New Year's Eve parties, I'd pictured having a quiet meal by ourselves, or playing board games with Joe and Noni, and then just Bobby and me sitting in front of the fireplace listening to our favorite music, waiting for midnight when we'd kiss and climb into bed under the warm quilts. We'd sleep as late as we wanted on New Year's Day and make breakfast together. Now, all there was to look forward to was the end of winter. A white plastic bag trapped on a fencepost flapped about like a cold ghost. *Stupid plastic bags.* Normally, I love winter, but this winter was reminiscent of *Dr. Zhivago*—all that snow. And the love triangle. As I drove into Holland, I listened as the sorrowful strains of *Lara's Theme* played over and over in my head. Could a love triangle be as heartbreaking as a father preferring to spend time with his son rather than his lover? I hoped I didn't have to find out.

Chapter 14

"Hannah. Mrs. DeGroot." Bobby nodded at the women standing inside the front door and took off his hat. "May we come in?"

The women backed up and Hannah motioned for Bobby and Al to enter. She closed the door behind them and asked what they wanted now. She appeared to be near exhaustion, and Bobby was sorry he had to be there. He asked if they could all sit because he had a few more questions.

"I know I should've been more honest with you about the horses. I'd like to explain if you'll listen." She looked steadily at Bobby, and as surprised as he was by what seemed her sudden turnaround to tell him the truth, he was skeptical. Sometimes what suspects thought of as truth was just another figment of their imagination. He had no choice but to listen. She invited them back to the kitchen to sit at the table. She didn't offer any beverage, which was fine with Bobby as he and Al had just left McDonald's.

"You're going to tell us why you stole Harvey Johnson's horses?" he began.

"Yes. Yes," she repeated and took a deep breath with a sigh of relief. She began what turned into a long monologue. "My mother loves horses. She was a famous circus performer at one time, a trick rider on horseback. You may not believe that, but it's true."

Bobby didn't interrupt by telling her he knew all about Edith Edna Severino's trick riding days. He suspected it wouldn't take much for Hannah to change her mind and clam up again. He waited patiently for her to finish, which she did after about fifteen minutes. In the meantime, Al stood quietly at the kitchen door listening to Hannah and watching Edith Edna's reactions as she sat at the kitchen table across from Hannah and Bobby.

"So you stole those horses because your mother loves horses and wanted to have horses nearby in the barn?"

"Well, yes, but it was more than that," she laughed incredulously. She looked at Bobby as if she was weighing how much to tell him. How much would this man believe? "You see, Sheriff, my mother felt Harvey Johnson was not taking good care of those horses. She even believed he was neglecting the horses. They weren't his after all. They were his father's." She paused. "My mother has Alzheimer's and she is hard to care for. I can't really do it by myself anymore. But, I thought if I could borrow Johnson's horses for awhile, she might get better, and she did for a spell. She spent time in the barn brushing them and feeding them. She even wanted me to call the farrier to come out and do their hooves. She can barely talk, but she made me look at one of the horse's hooves and said the word *farrier*. Then, she braided the one mare's mane with Christmas ribbon." Hannah was pleading now with Bobby, trying to make him understand why she stole the horses.

"But, surely you must have known you couldn't keep those horses. You knew we would find them."

"Have you ever taken care of someone you loved, Sheriff? Someone who needed you twenty-four hours a day? I'd do anything for Mom right now. Anything! I don't want my mother in some ten-story home for crazy people stacked up like cords of firewood," she hissed, tears now trickling down her face. "I just wanted to help her, even if it was just for a little while. I was away so long and didn't know she was getting sick 'til Daddy called. You don't know what it's like living out here with no help and no one to even talk to," she pleaded for him to understand.

"No, no, I don't, but it has to be hard." He said slowly as he remembered what Mary Jo had said about the corn not being picked. He decided to bring it up. "Hannah, did any of the neighbors offer to help you?"

"No. I don't think anyone knew Mom was this sick." She blew her nose and wiped her face with a rag she pulled out of her jeans pocket. Bobby looked around for a box of tissues and didn't see one.

"But, they knew your father had left. Didn't anyone offer to pick that field of corn to the east, or didn't you ever ask anyone to help you?"

Hannah looked puzzled. "No," she said. "People are busy and I didn't want to impose, and no one offered to help." She began to cry again. "I'm sorry, Sheriff. I know I shouldn't have taken the horses, but I had to do something to help my mom. It was wrong. I really don't even know what got into me. I know better. It did help her for a little while though. It did," she insisted.

Al pulled a small notebook and pen out of his jacket pocket and made a note to ask Harvey Johnson why he never offered to help Hannah pick her corn. Bobby felt sorry for Hannah, but he didn't believe her. At least, he believed she wasn't telling him the whole truth. She was holding something back.

"Okay, Hannah. We'll see if the Johnsons want to press charges." He pushed his chair back and stood up to go. "One more thing. What about the old horse left in Johnson's barn? Whose horse is that?"

Hannah again looked confused, and stalled by going to the kitchen sink and filling a glass with tap water. She turned back toward them and took a sip.

"You won't believe this. It's a little far-fetched," she hemmed and hawed leaning against the sink behind her. She breathed deeply through her nose and bit her lip before she began. "Mother was always suspicious. One of her suspicions was that horses with four white feet are evil, or dangerous, or whatever. I'm not sure. She hated that horse since the day Dad brought him home for her. Did you ever hear of an old saying that went something like, *One white foot—buy him; two white feet—try him; three white feet—look all about him; four white feet—go without him.* Supposedly, my mother had this ingrained in her from the time she started riding horses. It's crazy I know, but circus people have to be cautious and Mother would not go near that horse. It was so old, I figured Harvey Johnson would at least feed it, and if it died, Harvey has the means to bury it. I don't." She shrugged her shoulders like a teenager, and Bobby didn't know what to say. It seemed incredulous that a woman who loved horses would hate a horse because of four white hooves.

When he and Al got back into their SUV, Al flipped through his notebook and found the phone number for Harvey Johnson.

"Nope. Hannah DeGroot never asked for any help picking corn or anything else. As a matter of fact, I offered to pick that corn for her, and she refused me. Said she didn't want it picked. Said she was going to sell the farm and move with her mother back to Montana."

"Thanks, Mr. Johnson. We'll be in touch." Al ended the call.

They were still sitting in DeGroots' lane mulling over this information when Al asked if it was possible Mary Jo could be onto something. Was wanting to sell the farm a good enough reason not to have the corn picked? And Hannah obviously hadn't made any effort to move away or even put the farm on the market.

"Do we need a warrant to search a cornfield?"

Bobby wondered if somewhere deep in these snow white fields lay the bones of Harvey Johnson. He gazed out at the windswept fields with snow three feet deep and covering even the tallest cornstalk stubble. Canada geese darkened the sky as they took off from nearby farm ponds, their honks sounding like dogs barking.

"Call what's his name in Newtown and see when we can get some cadaver dogs out here. See if we can get them as soon as possible. Jim Travis is his name." Bobby would hate to miss the search for a body, but chances are a search wasn't going to result in finding a dead body. Yet, something told him it might.

"Roger that, Sheriff."

Chapter 15

My first stop was at home to let Archie out for a brief run in the yard while I changed into my work clothes, not that it mattered if I showed up in jeans. However, as a possible new owner of a book store, I wanted to look a little more professional.

As there didn't seem to be many shoppers about, I found a parking place right in front of The Nook. The "Help Wanted" sign was still in the window and reminded me I really needed to hire someone before Kevin went back to school full time. Kevin greeted me warmly, and I was happy to see him.

"Did anyone else apply for the job?" he asked after we'd begun unpacking a new shipment of books.

"Not yet. Only Lola VandeKamp."

"The blonde lady who chews gum?"

I looked at Kevin. "Well, yeah, I guess that does describe her. Funny that's what you remember about her."

"She was, like, very nice. Cool. You know."

I thought about Lola for a few seconds. The truth was I didn't like her much; but, if I was being honest, I had to admit it was only because she made a play for Bobby last May when Bobby and I were just starting to see each other. After Bobby explained the situation to her, she backed off. I hadn't seen her since.

"Really? You liked her and you think she'd be a good fit working here?"

"Sure, why not? It's not that many hours, and I'll still be here, like, whenever my classes allow."

Not knowing what else to do, I decided I'd give Lola a call and see if she was still interested in a part-time job working for me. I punched in the number she left on the application using the Nook's landline while thinking about my new smart phone still sitting in its box in the suitcase under the Christmas tree at home. With Bobby leaving town for a few days, I figured I'd have plenty of time to have Pippi help me get it set up and give me a lesson on the basics.

"Mary Jo! Is it really you? Do you really want me to work at the Nook? I can't believe it. I was just sitting here wondering what to do, and then the phone rings. I really need a job right now. Thank you, thank you, thank you." She said without taking a breath.

I warned her I couldn't pay her much, but she seemed fine with the meager salary and the short hours.

"When do you want me?"

"How about this afternoon? You could help us take down the Christmas tree and clean out the front window. It's not a glamorous job but it needs doing, and Kevin and I are in a mess right now." I looked around at the boxes of new books, the order forms, a dirty bakery display case and book shelves needing a good dusting. We settled on an arrival time of two o'clock, which would give her three hours of work and give me a chance to get some paperwork done. In the meantime, Kev and I began unpacking the new books.

I checked my wristwatch and looked out the display window just as an old El Camino pulled up and parked directly in front of the shop. Lola VandeKamp seemed to jump out of the driver's side and breeze through the door of the shop. Two o'clock sharp.

"I can't believe this, Mary Jo. I'm so glad you hired me. You won't regret it. I promise. What should I do first?" She cracked her gum.

I showed her where she could stow her coat and purse and asked her to fill out the usual employment paperwork. Lola once seemed beautiful to me, but now she looked sadly rundown—dark roots and brassy colored hair in need of a trim, a too-tight denim skirt topped with an out-of-date Christmas sweater, scuffed brown boots and Kevin was right, she was chewing gum constantly. The gum-chewing could become a problem for me, but for now, I didn't plan on bringing it up. I mainly wanted to get through the day without dwelling on Bobby leaving for Las Vegas in the morning. Training a new employee would help with that.

I gave Kevin the job of helping Lola clean out the front window and taking the Christmas tree down while I started cleaning up. One or two customers came in and browsed around. When one picked out a cookbook on the sale table, I had Lola come to the desk so I could show her how to ring up a sale. Kevin put Bobby's train set from the window display back in its original box and handed it to me.

"This is Sherriff Hanley's, isn't it?" Kevin asked.

"Just put it here behind the desk. I'll get it to him later. Thanks, Kevin." I was not going to let Bobby's train set remind me of how sweet he was to lend it to me.

A little later I overheard Lola asking Kevin if they stored the Christmas decorations here at the Nook. "Yes, Ma'am." He responded. Evidently, not wanting to be called ma'am, Lola shot back, "What? Do I look like your grandma?" Kevin just laughed.

In Holland, the days were short now. At four o'clock, I looked up from my book order to see that it was dark outside. The sky was gray and heavy. I knew I wasn't in the greatest mood, and I could see that Lola was trying her best. It wasn't Lola's fault Bobby chose to go to Las Vegas with his son instead of staying home to spend New Year's Eve with me. None-the-less, her gum-chewing was definitely getting on my nerves.

I asked Lola and Kevin if they thought we should rename the Book Nook to something else, and they were having a grand time thinking up ridiculous and some not-so-ridiculous names. Their laughter was lightening my mood when the door of the Nook opened with a tinkle of the little bell. A tall well-dressed man entered. Professor Oliver Burns was a stranger to Lola and Kevin, and they went silent as he stomped his boots on the black mat and removed his plaid wool paperboy cap. Professor Oliver Burns nodded a greeting to them and walked over to the desk with a rakish grin.

"You look busy, Mrs. McGee." His eyes seemed to drill into mine. I blinked without responding. "Would you please help me find another good book? A page-turner this time?"

"Sure. Follow me to the thriller section." I sensed him staring at my backside instead of the bookshelves. I spun around as soon as we reached the mystery section and pointed out Lee Child, Robert Baldacci, Robert Ludlum. "Are you sure this is what you want?" I couldn't quite picture the professor of French and romance languages reading these books.

"It is. It is. I need to be distracted for a few days." He paused. "Something to get me through New Year's Eve, you know." I did know. I smiled again. "Mary Jo, may I call you Mary Jo?" I nodded. "Do you mind if I ask if you're single? I noticed you don't wear a ring, so I thought you might be single, but everyone calls you Mrs. McGee. Are you? Single, I mean?"

"Um, yes, uh, I mean no." Not knowing how to explain and not wanting to, I stalled and he grinned. "It's complicated right now. I'm not married if that's what you mean."

"A boyfriend then?" he asked secretively.

"Yes, but I think he's moving away, so I guess I'll be unattached soon enough—not that I'm attached now. We just…well, you know. He's a good friend."

"Ah," he paused as if thinking deeply. "I was just wondering if you'd like to have dinner with me tomorrow night. It's the night before New Year's Eve and I'm free. On New Year's Eve I'll be flying to New York to visit friends. Hence, I need a good book for airport boredom." And then he lowered his voice, "And if you have dinner with me, I promise to keep it a secret from your boyfriend." He made air quotes with his fingers around *boyfriend* which rubbed me the wrong way.

"I'm not sure," I hesitated. "I don't normally go out on dates."

"Let's not call it a date then, and you have to eat, don't you? We'll call it a meal. Now, let me pay for these two books, and I'll be on my way. What time shall I stop by tomorrow then? Are you done here by five-thirty? An early dinner sounds good to me. How about Monarch's in the hotel?"

I must have nodded. He paid for his books and hurried out the door before I could think too much about what I'd just committed myself to. None-the-less, I refused to feel guilty. Bobby was leaving me alone for who knows how long, and I didn't think I had to sit home feeling sorry for myself. It was going to be just a meal after all.

I sent Lola home at five o'clock after ringing up the last customer, and Al came to pick Kevin up shortly after. I was hoping Kevin wouldn't say anything to Al about my date with Professor Burns. Maybe he didn't even hear the exchange although I doubted that. Lola and Kevin both seemed suddenly quiet while Professor Burns paid for his purchase. I waved at Al as Kevin ran out the door and leaped over the snow bank into Al's front seat. I looked around the Nook making sure Stella had food and water in her bowls, and admired the freshly dusted shelves and clean pastry case, which reminded me to tell Noni we needed some fresh sweets for it.

When I got home, it was dark. I let Archie out the door I had just come in, and we headed over to Joe and Noni's to see how they were doing, and maybe to confide in Noni about my upcoming nondate with Oliver Burns. I picked my way on the snow-packed path trying not to slip.

"You what?" yelled Noni when I told her of my plans.

"It's just a meal, Noni. Really. What are you thinking? That I'm going on a date behind Bobby's back?" I explained to Noni how I felt about Bobby going to Las Vegas two days before New Year's with Scott and Tennille. How I felt betrayed.

Noni just stared at me with her hands on her hips. Joe, who had been sitting at the kitchen table reading the newspaper quietly rose and walked into the living room closing the door behind him.

"Oh, so Bobby knows about it?"

I didn't say anything.

"So, he doesn't know. Mary Jo, this is not a good thing to do. Is Oliver Burns single?"

"Yes, of course, he's single."

"Then, this is going to be a date. Don't try to call it just a meal, and don't tell me you don't already feel guilty about it. I can see the guilt in your eyes. You love Bobby. Don't mess it up." She turned and started cutting up a pan of brownies. "By the way, you asked if I knew any place Lola V. might have been employed, and I remembered that she worked for Harvey Johnson at his tractor parts company. I think she got fired, but I'm not positive. Don't quote me on that. There was talk of Harvey Senior having an affair with Lola, and Jean Johnson, Junior's wife, putting an end to it because she didn't want Harvey Senior marrying a young woman, thereby delaying any inheritance they might receive from Harvey Senior upon his demise. Again, that might have been just rumors, but I'm pretty sure Lola worked for the company."

Affairs and rumors? I didn't know the Johnsons except for the occasional photo or article in the newspaper, but I knew I needed extra help at the store. Besides, I'd already hired Lola. She seemed to be working hard, and she and Kevin got along great. Actually, if Harvey Johnson, Sr. was divorced and Lola was divorced, could it really be called an affair?

"Those smell great, Noni. Are they for the Nook?"

"Of course, they're for the Nook. You can't see Joe and me eating a nine-by-thirteen pan of brownies by ourselves, can you?" She placed the brownies in a box lined with waxed paper and turned to face me. "Call Bobby and talk to him, Mary Jo. Don't wait for him to call you. Do you have your new phone with you?"

"Ah, no, I don't right now." I felt my coat pockets as if I normally carried it.

"It's not an instrument of the devil, Mary Jo. Bring it over and Joe can help you with it. In the meantime, go home and phone Bobby. Tell him you love him and you hope he has a wonderful trip and that you'll miss him. Go." She handed me the box of brownies looking up at me over her wire-rimmed glasses and pushed me toward the side door. "Put these in the fridge until the frosting sets, and call me tomorrow and let me know how you're doing. We'll be home all day. Joe's not feeling too good and plans to take it easy tomorrow. Don't slip on those steps," she cautioned.

I tried phoning Bobby when I got back inside my house, but only got his voice mail. I had no intention of telling him about my upcoming "meal" with Oliver Burns, and thought I would probably end up calling it off tomorrow anyway. I just left him a message to phone me when he had time. I wished I'd asked Al if they were at all concerned about the unpicked cornfield. There was probably a good reason why DeGroots didn't have it picked. I guessed that Bobby was busy packing for Las Vegas and would call me later in the evening. I couldn't fit the box of brownies in the fridge so left them on my back porch after removing one for myself. They'd freeze but that would be fine. Then, I went back inside and took my new iPhone out of its open-proof clamshell package. This took a serrated knife, a scissors and finally a can opener to cut through the plastic. Ten minutes to open my present. How much time it would take me to learn how to use the thing was mind-boggling.

I snarfed down the brownie as reward for getting the new phone out of its package. Baby steps I said to myself. I sat in my favorite chair staring at the Christmas tree with its lights and garlands and pinecones, remembering how when the girls were small Ron and I would sit and eat the cookies left for Santa knowing we'd done everything we could to make the holiday special for our children. It always seemed so peaceful, or was that just a trick my memory was playing on me? No use reminiscing, I thought. Times change. A new love might replace an earlier love, but the old love is always there, I knew. I wondered what my ex-husband was doing tonight out in sunny California. I turned on the reading lamp, grabbed the latest Louise Penny mystery off the coffee table and settled in for an evening of waiting for Bobby to return my call. I didn't have to wait long.

"Mary Jo. I'm glad I caught you." He sounded out of breath. "I wanted to come over and see you tonight but that can't happen now. You know I love you, don't you?" I told him *of course*, but deep inside I was beginning to have nagging doubts. "I hate leaving you right now, but I'll be back as soon as I can. Just not sure when that will be." He paused and seemed to take a deep breath. "Scott's in financial trouble. I don't know how bad it is. I think he has gambling debts, but he's being so damn elusive with me. I hate this, Mary Jo. I need to help him and Tennille, but I'm going to miss you. Tell me you understand, Red," he pleaded.

"Bobby, I don't know what to say. I do understand, of course. I'd do the same thing." As soon as I said this, I knew it was true. What wouldn't we do for our children? "Just do what you have to do. I'll be here when you get back. Do you have any idea when that will be?"

"I don't know at this point. Scott didn't even have health insurance to pay Tennille's hospital bill. On top of that, I have a feeling they don't even have a place to live. I won't be back until I can get some of that straightened out. What I'm thinking is that I might have to make more than this one trip out there, in which case, I'd come home soon, but I don't know. Hey," he changed the subject suddenly, "you might be on to something with the unpicked cornfield. We're getting a cadaver dog out there tomorrow morning, and we'll see if it picks up anything."

"Wow. Are you serious?"

"I am. Al thought it was questionable, too. I'll be on my way to Las Vegas, but Al and Jim Travis can handle everything."

"What time will they be out there?" The closest I'd ever been to a cadaver dog was the little beagle used at O'Hare to sniff out drugs. Have I mentioned that I love reading mysteries and envision myself quite the sleuth? I have a talent for skullduggery if I say so myself, so I was definitely intrigued by the idea of seeing a cadaver dog search for a, well, what else, a cadaver.

"Mary Jo. Do not even think about going out there." Could Bobby read my mind?

"I wasn't. I was just wondering. It is pretty exciting though."

"Yeah, I guess. I need to get going and get packed." I could hear the baby crying in the background. "One more thing, Red. I love you, and I'll be thinking of you."

"I love you too, Bobby. Stay safe. Let me know how it's going and if there's anything I can do to help."

"Will do. Just knowing you're in my life is a big help. Love you." He disconnected and I slowly pushed the "End" button. I looked at Archie lying by my feet. A cadaver dog, I said aloud. Archie looked up at me and tilted his head as if to say, "Huh?" I wondered what time that cadaver dog would be out at the DeGroot farm, and, what excuse I could give Al for just happening to be in the neighborhood.

Chapter 16

The sun hadn't even come up yet and maybe it wasn't going to, Al thought. Kevin sat at the kitchen table in Al's small house reading or studying a textbook.

"You're up bright and early for being on Christmas break. What's that?"

"Western Civ. Just thought I'd get a jump on it. I didn't do very good in high school. It just seems like everybody else at Central knows more than I do. Like they've been around more than I have."

Al pulled a chair out from the table and sat down. None of the chairs matched and the old maple table was covered in water-glass rings. Pippi planned to refinish it for him, which was a nice thought, but he knew it didn't matter what Pippi did or didn't do, he just plain loved her and loved having her in his life. She was good with Kevin too. Some women would resent his taking Kevin in and spending time with him, but not Pippi. Al wanted to correct Kevin and tell him he should have used "well" instead of "good," but he intuited this was not the time for a grammar lesson.

"Kev. You did great on your SATs, and Mrs. Donovan told me you could have done better in school if you'd had some encouragement from your folks. You know, you weren't having the same experiences as most of the kids in your classes, but that doesn't mean you're not as bright."

Kevin looked at Al and sighed.

"I know, Kev. Your father wasn't much of a father, and your stepmother betrayed you." Al wanted to put his arm around Kevin's shoulder, but hesitated. Teenagers don't like that, he thought. "Kevin, you don't have to be your past. You can be a better person than your father. Your stepmother is a sick person and you don't have to worry about her anymore. She's never getting out of prison. That is one guarantee I can make. Another guarantee is that I will do everything I can to help you. I remember a little about Western civilization. We can look at it later tonight, but right now, I need to get over to DeGroot's farm. Hey," he had a thought, "how would you like to come with me and see how a cadaver dog works?"

I stopped for a mocha latte at Aunt Harold's and headed out of Holland. The hot coffee and cold whipped cream combo perked me up after a restless night of dreaming about Bobby and worrying about him. Even with a girlfriend and new baby, Scott continued to be an irresponsible jerk. Now, he had taken Bobby away from me. But, driving out of town with a few flurries falling on the windshield, sipping my mocha made me feel like I was getting back in my groove. Getting my mojo back. I was the one who noticed the unpicked cornfield, who thought it was odd. Today, much to my surprise, it was being investigated. *I'm baack.* I started singing, "Get back. Get back. Get back to where you once belonged. Get back Jo Jo." The car had warmed up and I took off my mittens to get a better grip on both the steering wheel and the cardboard cup.

There was no other traffic as I drove carefully over the hills and around the curves on the snow-cleared county road. I spotted the barely plowed DeGroot lane and turned slowly into it. As I got closer to the house, I could see Al's deputy car and two other cars I didn't recognize. I slowed to a stop beside Al's and took one last sip of my mocha. I undid my seat belt and got out of the car. A biting wind greeted me, so I zipped up my parka as I wandered over to the propane tank and stood under a tree about thirty yards away from the cornfield. I watched several parka-clothed men and one woman wander slowly around the near edge of the field. Some poked sticks in the snow as they slogged through the thick white stuff. A dog ran unleashed between rows of corn. It slowed to sniff at smells unknown to humans. Then, it moved on. I knew I shouldn't be there, but I felt frozen to the spot and jumped when a clump of snow fell out of the tree onto my head.

"They'll find him soon." I turned to see who had spoken. A young woman with no coat stood shivering behind me hugging herself.

"What did you say?"

This had to be Hannah DeGroot. She looked to be in her forties so she clearly wasn't Edith Edna DeGroot, who I'd never met. She walked away from me, and I watched her go back inside the house. Al and someone who looked like Kevin started coming toward me from the field. The closer they got, I realized it was Kevin. I pulled my parka hood up over my head as we all exchanged pleasantries before Al asked me, in his business-like manner, what I was doing there. My explanation of never having seen a cadaver dog work, and Bobby telling me about it and the oddity of an unpicked cornfield being my idea in the first place all fell flat as soon as I'd said it. Then, I remembered what Hannah had said to me.

"But, Hannah DeGroot was just here, and she said you'd find him soon."

"She said what?" Al looked at me like I'd grown a second head.

"She said you'd find him soon. I'm sure that's what she said."

"Did you ask her who we would find?"

"No, she left as soon as she said it." I stamped my feet for warmth and told Kevin he could sit inside my car to warm up. At least the searchers were moving around. Standing still made my feet numb with cold and the wind seemed to be picking up as it blew snow in our faces. I could hardly make out the figures in the field, and I'd lost sight of the dog completely.

Al spoke, although I got the feeling he wasn't talking to me, but just thinking aloud. "Two men are missing—Harvey Johnson Sr. and Hannah DeGroot's father, Vince. Johnson has been missing since June and, from what Hannah told us, that was about the same time Vince DeGroot went missing." He looked at me, or maybe through me, and went on. "Supposedly, DeGroot left when his wife's Alzheimer's became too much for him to handle. I can sort of understand that, but what kind of man would desert his sick wife?"

"Al," I interrupted. "What happens if you find a body?"

"Oh, we might not find a body. We're just hoping to maybe find a clue out there. Anything. The Johnson family would like some closure, you know?"

"And justice too, I would imagine. If there was foul play, I mean."

"I hope we find something. The sheriff is kicking himself for not noticing the unpicked cornfield. Kudos to you, Mary Jo. I mean Ma'am."

I wanted to tell Al to stop calling me "ma'am," but the dog was barking and people were running in its direction. Al took off toward the field with me behind him. We slipped and slid all the way tripping over snow-buried weeds and rocks. Men in parkas and a barking dog were cloistered around a lump on the ground among the corn stalks. I could only make out a brown fabric before Al turned around and suggested I get back to my car.

"Please, Mary Jo, we'll do this by the book and that does not include having a civilian witness this. Go on now. Bobby wouldn't want you here. You know that."

I backed up and turned to go. Al was right. I didn't belong here. It reminded me of last spring when I found myself trapped in a barn with a madwoman. I cringed and hauled myself back up to my car where I stood with Kevin for a few minutes. Then a woman, who I guessed to be Hannah DeGroot, came running out the front door of the house with no coat or boots on—just faded jeans, a plaid flannel shirt and tennies. I took off running trying to catch up with her, but couldn't. We both reached the commotion at the same time. Corn stalks lay stamped flat in the snow. The circle of men parted, and there it was. I saw ribs and hoped it was just a deer injured on the road who found a quiet place to die. Then, I saw the faded blue overalls frozen to the corpse. One arm absent of flesh stretched outward. I didn't see the face but imagined there was not much left to see.

Hannah started crying. Then we both were pulled away, but not before Hannah screamed something I couldn't make out. It sounded like, "He looks human. He looks human." She kept screaming it. Al took her arm, and she went somewhat willingly with him back to the house. The cadaver dog's trainer led it away, hopefully, for a "good job" treat. I followed Al and Hannah up the incline toward the house. She had to be freezing, and Al urged her on. Another deputy caught up with them. Al told him to call for an ambulance and notify the county coroner's office. Then he added, "He might want to meet the ambulance at the morgue. Get the state troopers to send a technician and a crime scene van. I'll be inside with Hannah. Can you wait for them in your car and show them the body when they get here?"

Al turned to me and smiled. "Good job, Mary Jo. Noticing the corn hadn't been picked, I mean. Can you take Kevin home for me, or better yet, is he supposed to work today? That would be good for him, I think. To be with you at the Nook."

I nodded sure and looked to the house. An old witch's face stared out at me from a dirty window pane. It scared me more than seeing the bones in the field. I turned and headed for my car.

Before I left, two TV news trucks pulled into the farm lane and stopped before they got to the house. I shouldn't have been surprised. Holland is a small community, and Des Moines is less than an hour away. I grabbed Kevin who was waiting at my car. He looked pale but assured me he was okay.

My shoes were soaked and my toes were numb by the time Kevin and I arrived at the Nook. At some point on our drive back into town, I remembered my dinner engagement that evening with the professor, and realized I'd have to run home to change my clothes before closing time. I was regretting my decision to go out to eat. After seeing a corpse in a cornfield and seeing Hannah's reaction, I felt a little sick. Was the corpse Hannah's father or was it Harvey Johnson? Al said something about getting a technician and the crime scene unit out to the farm. An autopsy would have to take place. How long would that take? What had Hannah said when she'd seen the body? *He looks human*? Would Al have heard her say that? I needed to phone Al to tell him what I heard. Unfortunately, the Book Nook was busy all morning. Lola made a dramatic entrance a full hour early. She was outfitted in a black velvet warm-up suit with sequins. She had plucked her eyebrows down to a few hairs and penciled in dark brows.

"I came in early because I was ready, and I can stay late, too."

"Oh, happy day." I smiled nastily and immediately felt guilty. She came in early, the shop is busy, so get over it I told myself. "Great!" I said. "That's great."

Kevin helped Lola ring up sales and make a refund to a woman who "didn't like the book." When things had quieted, they shared tuna salad sandwiches Lola had brought. I took advantage of the lull and ran home to change into something more presentable for dinner. This took longer than I'd anticipated. When I returned to the Nook, Kevin and Lola were reorganizing the children's area and, I had to admit doing a fine job of it. Lola eyed my teal blue sweater, the black skirt and knee-high black boots critically, but didn't say anything—just cracked her gum a half dozen times and turned away. I wondered if she remembered I had a date with Professor Burns. I sent her home at four o'clock. She looked tired, and we had no customers.

"I wouldn't like to live in her head, but she's okay." Kevin grinned. "She came up with a great name for the Nook," he looked at me closely and slowed his speech, "if you still want to change it."

"And what would that be, Kevin?" I raised an eyebrow at him.

"The Dutch word for book shop."

"Which is?"

"Well, we didn't take the time to, like, google it, but we could now." He got out his iPad, a Christmas gift from Al and Pippi, and began finger-tipping the screen.

"Got it. It's *boek winkel.*"

"*Boek Winkel? Boek Winkel,*" I repeated wondering if I was pronouncing it correctly. "I like that. I really like that, Kevin." We stood there smiling at each other until I told him he could take off early, too. I knew he had basketball practice and could easily catch a ride with a friend or walk to campus, and I was feeling uncomfortable about the professor showing up to take me to dinner. What would we have in common? What would we talk about? Well, my experience out at the DeGroot farm that morning would be interesting. It's not everybody who sees a cadaver dog find a dead body in a cornfield.

At five o'clock I hung the "Closed" sign in the window, turned off a few lights and waited for the professor. I wished I'd called it off. Now, it was too late unless I feigned being sick, and who would believe that? With that thought, I heard the bell on the door tinkle, and in walked Professor Oliver Burns looking quite dapper in a brown tweed overcoat, a green muffler and a red and brown plaid hat that could only be described as a Sherlock Holmes hat. He removed the hat and bowed in greeting. I couldn't help but laugh. He explained that it was a gift from an exchange student from Britain. I guessed the student was female and wondered if the professor was a ladies' man.

He helped me with my coat and I wrapped my warm scarf tightly around my neck, deciding at the last minute to wear my warm fleece hat. I'd wanted to look nice for the evening, but it was cold and windy and no man was worth an earache or head cold. I locked the front door, and we started walking toward the Royal Amsterdam Hotel. The mercury had plummeted, and I pointed out the time and temperature sign on the bank. *Twelve degrees.* A lot of snow for the end of December. We agreed it was good for snow removal businesses as we crossed Franklin and walked through the Franklin Place alley. Beneath my boots, I could see the red bricks where snow had been scraped off making it somewhat slick. The professor took my arm, and I was glad I had my flat boots on. He talked nonstop about his day and about a book he thought I'd like. I needn't have worried about lack of conversation. We turned left at the Molengracht Canal and hurried across the bridge with the wind blowing at our backs.

Chapter 17

That's incredible, Al. Just incredible. I wish I was there."

"It's okay, Sheriff. Not a problem. I had plenty of help. I'm just glad the dog found it. The body I mean. I mean how long must it have been buried out there?" Al was a little nervous about Mary Jo being out at the crime scene. He knew Bobby wouldn't like that she was and, for now, Al figured Bobby didn't have to know.

"More important, whose body is it? Harvey Johnson or Vince DeGroot? Did you get any feel for that?"

"Negative. The body was partially decomposed. Dr. Van Zee plans to do an autopsy Monday. Hannah was screaming something but no one knew what. She was incoherent."

"Not til Monday? Hmm, I suppose because tomorrow is New Year's Eve and Sunday is New Year's Day. Maybe I can be back by then. Did Hannah say anything? Give you any sign that she knew that body was out there?"

"Negative, Sheriff. She clammed up when I got her back inside. She knows something though. I think she's protecting someone. Maybe her mother? Her relationship with truth is suspect, I think. I don't know, but I want to talk to her again."

"Al, go back out there first thing tomorrow and see if she'll talk." Bobby wished he was there to do it himself, but he knew Al was a skilled and thoughtful investigator and could handle it. "Take somebody with you. I should get goin', Al. I'm out here in the Neon Sign Museum—a boneyard of antique neon signs that used to be on all the old casinos. Vintage Americana, Al." He paused. "I'm trying to get Scott out of debt and back on his feet, but I wish I was there to help you. Thanks for the update, Al. Call me when you find out anything else."

"Roger that, Sir." Al had wanted to reassure his friend and boss, but didn't really know how to do that without making it sound like Bobby wasn't needed. He hoped he wouldn't let his boss down.

If Bobby smiled at Al's closing, it wasn't because he found Al's strictness to the rules and his by-the-book way funny or odd. No, it was because Bobby loved Al and, if he was honest with himself, he loved Al as much as he loved his own son, Scott, maybe more. Losing his friend, DCI Agent Frances Curoe, last May to a shooter as she was helping him investigate a murder shook him to the core. She had been a few months away from retirement, and he couldn't get her funeral out of his mind. Now, he was close to retirement and was glad of it. The thrill, the exhilaration he used to get when solving a case was no longer there. Just the opposite. He was unhappy with the job, and knew it was time to leave. Al's news of finding a body in DeGroots' cornfield would normally have excited him, but now Bobby just felt tired and worried. Worried about Al getting into something evil and dangerous.

Chapter 18

The hotel restaurant was decorated beautifully for the holiday season. I'd always loved little fairy lights in garlands of fresh evergreens. We were seated at a window overlooking the canal, and I started to thaw in the warmth of the room. Oliver ordered a bottle of Cabernet without asking me what I wanted, and we scanned our menus. He put on his reading glasses and seemed to study the menu. I missed Bobby, but was determined to have a good time.

"So many choices," he said without looking up. "Grilled lemon prawns. Dutch shredded beef with cabbage. Macadamia-crusted prime rib with mashed potatoes and asparagus sounds good. What would you like, Mary Jo?"

Well, at least he asked, but these dishes were priced out of my budget, and I was too polite to stick a date with a large bill, so I was determined to pick something good, but not extravagant. I was also well aware of the holiday pounds my body had started to gain, without permission, since Thanksgiving. I ended up ordering salmon with a baked potato. Oliver told the waitress we'd order a cheese course and dessert later. I glanced at the dessert menu which listed Pavlova with strawberries as the special. I knew Pavlova was a meringue and might be the lowest calorie dessert on the menu. I found myself wishing we could cut to the chase and just eat our dessert and head home. While we waited for our dinners, Oliver pulled his cell phone out of his pocket and spent the time checking his messages. The evening seemed to stretch out interminably.

Our dinners were served and Oliver made a comment about my baked potato being served in tin foil which evidently wasn't up to his standards, but it tasted good to me. He complained his food was too rich. I ate while listening to Oliver tell me about his childhood, his college days, his car, his ex-wife and just about everything without once asking me anything about myself. I, in turn, tried to enjoy the ambiance of the restaurant. It was furnished in the European style making me feel like I was traveling abroad. The dark oak paneling was rich and comforting, and there was candlelight on every table. Most of the tables sat empty, but I knew when the college was in session, parents of students often stayed at the hotel and the restaurant did a good business.

Oliver refilled my glass with wine, and I took a sip. It tasted better now that I had some food in my stomach. I thought of what I'd witnessed that morning at the DeGroot farm and wanted to tell someone about it. I wanted to talk to Bobby about it, but Oliver would have to do. Just as I cleared my throat and started to tell him, he scraped the last bit of crème brulee out of the dish, put his elbows on the table, tented his hands and said, "You don't mind if it's Dutch treat, do you Mary Jo? It's pretty much how my circle of friends does things."

The question stunned me, and I couldn't speak for what seemed like an hour. He'd said "circle of friends" with a somewhat snooty air that I didn't like. I wanted so badly to say something smart and snooty myself, but only came out with, "Of course not," as I pulled my wallet out of my purse and asked him

what I owed. He told me the total amount but said it would be fine if I only paid for the food.

"I'll cover the drinks and tip. How's that?" He looked at me inquiringly while cracking his knuckles.

Be still my heart. "Sure," I replied withdrawing into myself. *Why had I come*? I wondered what Bobby was doing in Las Vegas with Scott and Tennille and baby Noelle. I just wanted to get back to the Nook and get in my car and drive home to see Archie. It was plenty early. I could still get home and call Bobby. After paying my share of the bill and getting our coats on, we headed outside and back toward the Book Nook. The wind had died down and flakes as big as white moths were falling, but I couldn't appreciate their beauty. When we got to my car, I unlocked it and quickly got out the snow brush, but before I could begin scraping off snow, Oliver pulled me to him holding me too tightly. He pressed his mouth over mine. Then, he stood back and let go of me.

"Look, I've got to run but I'll call you when I get back from New York. How's that?"

I didn't want him to call me back ever, but before I could say anything, he was walking hurriedly down the street away from me. Guess I don't have to worry about hurting his feelings, I thought.

Pulling into my driveway with the wipers making a fan-shaped design on the snowy windshield, I noticed Joe and Noni's garage door open. It struck me as odd because they never left their garage door open at night. The pine trees groaned from the weight of the snow as I waded through the heavy stuff to their front porch. I rang the doorbell and waited. Surely they wouldn't be in bed this early. I peeked through the window in the door. The whole house looked dark. I walked back to their garage to pull the door down for them. Noni's little Fiesta was inside and Joe's blue Silverado pickup was in the driveway. Well, they must be home and in bed already, I reasoned, and headed over to my house.

Archie greeted me at the side door with yips of joy before rushing out into the snow and rolling around in it. Golden retrievers love snow and Archie was no exception. I kicked my boots against the doorframe to knock off the snow. I stepped inside, turning on the kitchen light, and saw the red light blinking on my phone. A message from Bobby was my first thought, but it was a frantic-sounding Noni instead.

"Mary Jo, when you get home, call me. No, come to the hospital. Joe's sick. I'm going to the hospital with him. Oh, in the ambulance. They're giving him oxygen. Yes, yes." She was breathless and I heard voices in the background—voices that sounded business-like, yet urgent. The message was left at six-fifteen and it was now eight-thirty. I grabbed my purse and headed back out the door. A snow-covered Archie waited for me.

"Sorry, Arch. You have to stay home this time. I'll make it up to you tomorrow with a long walk." He hung his head and flopped down on his favorite rug. I gave him a few treats for being a good boy.

I was standing at the hospital's information desk in less than twenty minutes. "Joe Donovan," I repeated. "He was brought in by ambulance a couple of hours ago."

Finally, the receptionist called for someone to take me to a waiting room. It held four cushioned chairs and one lamp table covered with ragged magazines. Noni sat slumped over in one of the chairs with her chin on her chest. She looked up when she heard me enter. For the first time since I'd known her, she finally looked her age. Ashen and with the corners of her mouth sagging, she seemed to be in a state of shock. Pain showed in her eyes, but she wasn't crying.

"Noni," I sat in the chair next to her and took her hand. "What happened?" I asked softly.

She nervously told me how Joe hadn't felt well for a couple of days. How she felt so bad for not taking it seriously. I tried to tell her we are all guilty of doing that, but she couldn't be consoled. She told me he couldn't eat any dinner, and went into their bedroom to rest, and how, when she went in to check on him, he was in pain and short of breath. She called 911 and waited for them. Then, she smiled and said they were there in less than five minutes. I wondered if that was true, but it didn't matter.

"Where is he now, Noni? Can we see him?"

"Oh, no, not now. They rushed him into surgery. It's a heart attack, Mary Jo." She started to cry a little. "He's eighty-four. Can you save an eighty-four-year-old man?" I fished in my purse for a tissue and handed it to her. She blew her nose and surprised me by saying rather loudly, "The old coot. He hates doctors and he worked too hard and he ate too much, but I love him. I love him so much. I don't know what I'd do without him."

I hugged her as she told me the surgery could last six hours. She wasn't sure it had even started yet, but they said they'd let her know. They'd had to call in an on-call emergency heart surgery team.

"I know you're scared, Noni, but I'll stay with you 'til it's over. Can I phone your kids for you?"

"I'm not scared of anything I can run from, Mary Jo, but that list gets shorter each year." She gave me her old devilish grin, but then her face turned sad. "This isn't something I can run from, is it?" She looked at me with exhausted eyes. "I told the kids I'd call them when he got out of surgery—when there was something to tell."

I nodded and consoled her as best I could, and even told her about finding a body out on the DeGroot farm that morning. The oddness of that didn't seem to register with her as a nurse came in and asked us to follow her to a more comfortable waiting room. It was larger and, again, it was vacant, but we now had two large sofas in addition to several chairs. I convinced Noni to lie down on one of the overstuffed sofas, and we settled in for a long wait.

Soft voices woke me. Opening my eyes to the artificial light from a table lamp, I remembered where I was. I guessed it was a doctor sitting next to Noni. He was saying something about ninety percent blocked and eighty percent blocked. My heart sank and I must have gasped or moaned. They both looked at me. Joe's surgeon introduced himself to me.

"Are you the daughter?"

"No. I'm just their neighbor. I mean best friend. I'm Noni's friend and neighbor," I stammered. "Is Joe..." I didn't want to say the word. He smiled and turned back to Noni.

"Joe's fine for the moment. The surgery was successful. I was just explaining to Mrs. Donovan that he had four occluded, or blocked, arteries, so we had to do a quadruple bypass. We took some veins from his legs so he'll have two incisions on each thigh, and one large incision on his chest. I can take you to the recovery room if you'd like to see him, but then he'll sleep most of the night. He won't know you're here so I'd recommend you take Mrs. Donovan home to get some rest. She can come back in the morning. How does that sound?" He looked at Noni, who was still sitting on the sofa clutching her purse and a hanky.

"I'd like to see him first and then maybe I would like to go home to rest." She looked at me for confirmation and I nodded. I knew she would need a good night's rest, which is nearly impossible in any hospital.

The surgeon led the way down the corridor, up four or five steps, through a huge waiting room with people sprawled about on chairs and sofas, then through two doors, where we were asked to wash our hands at a sink. The surgeon, who I now regarded as a hero, told us the nurses would take it from here as he waved good-bye to us. We were led to one of several beds in the huge recovery room. A nurse stood over a sleeping Joe Donovan. Aside from various tubes protruding from his nose, arm and out from under the sheet, he looked like Joe. Noni finally reacted with tears. The caring nurses talked to her about Joe's condition and what to expect in the coming days. I looked at my watch. It was two o'clock in the morning. New Year's Eve day. I thought of Bobby and wondered what he was doing when I realized a nurse was talking to me.

"Can you take Mrs. Donovan home? We've decided it would be best for her to get some sleep before coming back in the morning."

"Noni, is that all right? You do look like you could use some rest, and I can bring you back any time tomorrow. You want to call your kids now, don't you?"

Noni agreed and so we left Joe in the competent care of the nurse in charge, who promised she'd phone Noni if there was any change in Joe's condition. We found our coats and headed down to the main entrance leaving the awful lights of a hospital behind us. I had Noni wait at the door while I walked to my car. I turned the heat dial to high and hit the defrost button.

I helped Noni into the car and got out my new iPhone, thinking we could call one of her kids. My thought was whichever one we reached could call the other three. They all lived out of state, but their daughter lived in Kansas City and could be here in three hours if need be. I hit the button on my phone, but the screen stayed black.

"Let me see it," Noni said guessing I hadn't taken the time to learn anything about my new phone. "It's dead, Mary Jo. You need to recharge these things once in awhile."

"Dead? I haven't even used it yet. How can it be dead?"

Noni explained the facts of life to me as we headed home. *So that's what that little cable thing was for. Maybe Bobby had tried to phone me and couldn't get me.* I wished I'd brought my old phone, and was irritated at modern technology, yet grateful there was a possible reason for not hearing from Bobby.

I pulled into Noni's driveway and walked her to the side door offering to spend the night with her. She wouldn't hear of it. She wanted to phone her daughter and she promised she'd crawl into bed as soon as she reached her daughter or one of her boys. She said she'd phone me if she heard from the hospital in the night. Otherwise, I was to pick her up at eight a.m. to take her back to the hospital.

The feeling of being wrung through a wringer hit me as soon as I walked into my house. My head hurt and my mind felt inhabited by a dancing dervish. I couldn't decide what to do first. Charge my new phone. Let Archie out. Take a hot bath. Eat something? Yes. Set alarm for seven. Would that give me enough time? I should call Pippi. No, too late. Was that really a kiss the professor gave me or had he just slipped on ice and caught himself by grabbing me? Did I really see a dead body out at that farm this morning? Technically, that was yesterday morning. This is Saturday morning, New Year's Eve day.

I let Archie out one last time before bed. Warm tears flooded my eyes as I made a cup of tea and some toast. Killian had shown me how to make a good *cup o' tea*. "Don't use a microwave," he'd warned. "And don't be boilin' the water. Ye don't want bubbles." The thought of Killian being in prison overwhelmed me. I knew then I'd give anything to have Bobby here to talk with. *Anything including moving to Las Vegas?*

Chapter 19

Bobby's cell phone startled him awake at six a.m.

"Good morning, Sheriff. Happy New Year's Eve Day."

"Mornin', Al," he yawned as he sat up on the lumpy mattress in his Best Western motel room. Scott and Tennille and the baby were safe for the time being in Tennille's mother's small apartment in Henderson. "What's up?"

"I'd like to run something by you before I drive out to DeGroots' this morning."

"Go ahead." Bobby thought about asking if it could wait an hour or two, but it was already eight a.m. Central Standard Time back home, and he knew Al was always ready to go the minute he started his shift.

"Sheriff, even without an autopsy report, we know that body will be either the missing Harvey Johnson Sr. or Vince DeGroot, who appears to be missing even though no one reported him missing. Either way, foul play is indicated, and I just want to run the list of suspects by you if that's okay."

"Sure, Al. What are you thinking?"

"We know Hannah DeGroot is a suspect, because she stole Johnson's horses. We just don't know what her motive for killing him would be; but we know the DeGroots are down on their luck right now and they obviously need money. You mentioned the cost of putting the mother in an Alzheimer's facility, and they don't even have money to buy food. Pippi told me they're on food stamps."

"I'm sorry to hear that," Bobby said thoughtfully. "I feel bad for Hannah, but you need to question her about their finances. Harvey Jr. told me that selling healthy horses to Canada for horsemeat is a very profitable business. That's motive for stealing those horses, but not for murdering the horses' owner. I feel like we're missing something, Al. You got anything else?"

"Well, yes. I was thinking about Harvey Junior too. He has a motive for killing his old man because of the inheritance he would receive. His wife, Jean, is a suspect, too, because of that inheritance. They are definitely not living the lifestyle of the rich and famous. And, I don't think we can rule out the twin daughters as suspects. Teenagers are capable of committing murder and, sometimes, have killed a parent or grandparent. They don't like the house rules or they've been abused or whatever." Al knew that sounded a little far-fetched, but was taught by Bobby to expect the unexpected and be prepared. "I just wish we knew how Johnson died if, in fact, it is Johnson's body."

"We'll have to wait on the autopsy, Al, but remember when we first questioned Johnson's neighbors and coworkers last June, when he first went missing, no one had a kind thing to say about him. Keep that in mind when you're questioning Hannah, and keep it in mind when you're questioning Harvey Junior. He was protecting his wife when I asked to talk with her last week. Let me know how it goes. Call me on my cell day or night." He paused but Al knew he wasn't finished. "I've got plans with Scott today. I think we've found a new job for him that doesn't involve the casinos. Seems he can't be around gambling without getting into a game himself. Anyway, I'm hoping to get that squared away today and be back home soon."

"Sounds good, Sheriff." Al hoped that was true. He missed Bobby and hoped Scott could learn to stand on his own feet now that he had a baby and a steady girlfriend.

"Oh, and Al? Have you seen Mary Jo?"

"No, I didn't see her yesterday, but Kevin worked all afternoon with her at the Nook. He said he helped her get her new smart phone set up and working. I bet she'll call you on it today." Al neglected to tell Bobby that if Kevin was right, Mary Jo had a date last night with a professor from Central College. Al would confirm that with Pippi later, because Pippi usually knew what her mother was up to.

"Great. Thanks, Al. Oh, find out from the Johnsons just how big their inheritance would be if that body does turn out to be Harvey Senior."

"Will do. Ten four, Sheriff."

As Al headed out to the DeGroot farm, he went over a mental list of motives for murder. Sometimes people kill to protect someone, he thought. Because there were not many murders committed in Jasper County, he didn't have the experience for solving a murder case. Plus, if this really was a murder, the Iowa DCI would be called in for help. Wouldn't it be great if I solved this case before Bobby returned and before the DCI got involved, he pondered. Motives were many. They varied from the three big Ls—love, lust, and loathing—to other more common motives like revenge or greed or crimes of passion where the killer often doesn't even remember killing someone. He immediately thought of Edith Edna DeGroot and the fact that she had Alzheimer's disease; but, what could be her motive? Would an old woman even have enough passion to commit murder? Then he remembered Mrs. DeGroot was much younger than she appeared. He tried to remember her age. Mid-sixties was as close as he could figure. He slowed the Jeep as he neared the snow-covered DeGroot lane. *Could Edith Edna DeGroot be a suspect*?

Too late he remembered that Bobby had told him to bring someone with him when he questioned Hannah DeGroot.

Chapter 20

The alarm woke me at seven. With his snout resting a few inches from my face looking concerned, that is, if dogs can look concerned, Archie stood close to the bed. The furnace clicked on and hummed softly while my mind shifted into gear.

"We have to get Noni to the hospital, Arch. No snowshoeing this morning. Maybe later." I wasn't sure there would be many customers at the Nook on New Year's Eve, but most of the stores were open. Some would close early, and I hoped that would work for me, too. My plan was to take Noni to the hospital and then call Bobby to tell him about Joe. The thought of phoning Bobby made me nervous. I couldn't help but wonder why he hadn't phoned me. I glanced at my new iPhone on the night stand expecting to see a green light or something telling me it was charged, but maybe iPhones don't do that. At least, I now knew how to turn it on. Now, I saw the one hundred percent charged image, but there was still the two-hour time change between here and Las Vegas to consider. Bobby was an early riser, but five a.m. was too early to phone anyone. I eased myself out of bed and showered while planning what to wear. Then I got dressed and quickly ate an apple while Archie did his business outside.

The sun was trying to break through gray clouds, but flurries fell lightly on my bare head as I trod carefully on my slippery driveway to the garage. While backing my Honda out and closing the garage door, in my rearview mirror, I spotted Noni coming out her side door. She was dressed warmly and looked smaller than usual with huge brown furry earmuffs covering her ears.

"A Christmas present, Noni?" I asked nodding at her earmuffs as she got into the car. I'd meant to get out and open the door for her, but she was too quick.

"Sally sent them to me a couple of weeks ago when I'd complained about not having a hat warm enough to keep the cold wind out of my ears." She laughed a little as I backed the car into the street. We talked about every mundane thing we could talk about with no mention of Joe. I didn't think this was necessarily a good thing, and yet Noni seemed to enjoy talking about her kids and grandkids. She was anxious for her daughter, Sally, to arrive and asked if I'd heard from Bobby. We laughed some more about my not knowing how to use an iPhone. "Phone him, Mary Jo, or phone me first to make sure you know how to phone someone." I told her I would definitely phone her later in the day to see how Joe was doing.

By the time I dropped her off at the hospital's front door, parked my car and returned to the hospital entrance, she had disappeared. I headed to the CCU where Joe had been last night and found Noni standing by Joe's side as a nurse helped him swing his legs over the side of the bed and sit up. His face scrunched in pain, but he smiled at me. With tears in my eyes, I smiled back. The nurse told us Joe would be moved to a private room that afternoon. We talked for a few more minutes before the nurse hinted I was disrupting her plans to get Joe on his feet. I hugged Noni and whispered in her ear I'd be at the Nook most of the day and to call me if she needed anything.

"Not to worry, Mary Jo. Sally will be here by noon for sure." Her fine white hair clung statically to the earmuffs as she reached up and removed them. I felt a huge wave of compassion and concern for both her and Joe, and refused to think of what my life would be like without them. A nurse was helping Noni out of her coat as I turned and walked backwards out the swinging door.

The sky had darkened with clouds and flurries fell increasingly by the time I pulled into a parking spot close to the Nook. The winter air was dry and frigid giving the morning a pristine feel and, as I looked up and down the street, I saw how peaceful and lovely Holland was. I breathed in that special air and looked forward to some time alone in the Nook to organize things and relish the quietness. I didn't spot Stella when I first entered, so I climbed the stairs to Killian's old apartment and found the pretty yellow cat sleeping in the middle of Killian's old bed. She opened one eye to see who was disturbing her, and closed it when she saw it was just me.

"I'll be downstairs if you need anything, Girl." I said.

"Whatever," I imagined her saying.

"Lola, you mean you dated Harvey Johnson, Sr., the missing man?"

"Sure. I was single. My swine of a husband divorced me. I was free, and Harvey was separated from his wife. Poor woman. Harvey Johnson may have been rich at one time, but he gambled like crazy, and he treated Bernadette like dirt. A real ladies man type. Thought he could buy people." Lola was chewing her gum with a vengeance. "But, you know, I think she might have deserved it. She's no saint either. You know? I don't think she loved Harv. I think she loved the things Harv could buy her." Lola cracked her gum thoughtfully. "Bernie's her name. Well, she always wanted to be called Bernadette, but to me, she was just Bernie."

"So, Harvey Johnson was pretty wealthy?" I was getting intrigued.

"Couldn't prove it by me. He never spent a dime on me. Just wanted to come over and have sex." She looked secretively over at Kevin, who was trying to sweep up the slush that our first customers of the morning had tracked in. She whispered to me, "He wasn't all that good in bed either. Elvis had left the building, if you know what I mean." She winked at me. I didn't know what she meant.

"No. What do you mean?"

"He couldn't—you know." She again looked over at Kevin, who was now openly listening to Lola's every word. "Honestly, Mary Jo, he needed Viagra or something to, you know, perform."

Kevin hooted loudly, and I soon joined in. For the life of me, I hoped I'd never hear anyone ever say, "Elvis has left the building" again. I wanted more information about Lola's time spent with Harvey Senior, so questioned her some more. It seemed they mostly went to casinos out of town where Lola would play the slots—with her own money thank you very much—while Harvey would play poker and blackjack. Eventually, Harvey would come find her and take her home. Lola knew when he'd had a bad night, and the bad nights far outnumbered the good nights according to her. I thought this was interesting news and wondered if Bobby and Al knew about Johnson's gambling. Then I heard a sound I'd never heard before. I looked around. Lola and Kevin were staring at me.

"Isn't that your phone, Mary Jo?" Lola asked chewing her gum loudly.

I spun around. My new phone. Where's my new phone? I ran to my purse behind the counter and dug into the mess of tissues, lipsticks, my wallet, and finally dumped all the purse's detritus onto the counter and found the impatient phone. *Now what*? I just stared at that thing not knowing what button to push. Kevin and Lola appeared on either side of me. Lola grabbed the phone from me, but by then, the ringtone had stopped. She cracked her gum.

"Maybe they'll leave a message. You can check and see who it was." They showed me how to check and it turned out to have been Pippi. I should have phoned her earlier, but I'd lost track of time and now wished I'd tried phoning Bobby, too. I decided to phone Bobby first. Kevin showed me how to push the icon called "Phone" and then "Keypad." Now, as I punched in Bobby's number, I remembered what it felt like in kindergarten not knowing what all those letters on the board meant. He didn't answer.

"Shoot!" I said to no one in particular.

"You could, like, text him," Kevin encouraged. I just looked at him.

"I don't know how to text." I shook my head disgusted with myself.

"I'll do it for you if you want. Just tell me what you want to say."

"Ah, thanks, Kevin. I don't know. I'll just try him later, I think. But, thanks. If my phone rings again, can you show me what to do?" Just then, my phone rang. The number displayed was Pippi's. Kevin pushed the icon "Accept" and handed the phone to me.

"Mom. I can't reach Al. I spent the night at his house, and he left about eight this morning to go see Hannah DeGroot out at their farm, and he won't pick up. I'm a little worried. Maybe a lot worried. I don't know. I wouldn't worry except I've tried umpteen times to call him. I've texted him, too."

"You know how to text?" I asked.

"Sure. Doesn't everybody? Well, I mean everybody under the age of…" Pippi paused probably trying to remember my age. "It doesn't matter. I'll show you how to text sometime, but I'm not sure if I should be concerned about Al, or if I should just call headquarters and ask them. I don't want to embarrass him. It's probably nothing. It's just a little unusual, you know?"

"Don't worry, Pippi. Al can take care of himself." But, even as I said these words, I wasn't sure they were true. I saw Hannah DeGroot yesterday looking like a crazy person. I saw Edith Edna DeGroot in the window looking like the Wicked Witch of the

North. And, not to put too fine of point on it, I also saw a dead body on their grounds. "There's something else I wanted to tell you this morning. Don't get upset because I think it's going to be okay but… ."

"Mom! What?"

"Well, Joe had a heart attack late last night. Noni called 911 and an ambulance took him to Holland Regional."

"Oh, no. Oh, no. Joe? Oh, my God. Mom, how is he? What's happened?"

I told Pippi all about Joe's quadruple bypass surgery and that I saw him this morning looking better. Also, that Noni was handling it as well as could be expected and that their daughter was on her way here to be with Noni. When Pippi was satisfied with all the information I could give her, she asked me again what I thought she should do about Al.

I looked at Lola and Kevin who were busy straightening the shelved books. Business had been slow all morning, which helped me arrive at a decision I'd later regret.

"Pippi, I'll pick you up at Al's in ten minutes, and we can be at DeGroots in another ten."

Chapter 21

Al made a quick decision and swung his Jeep around the way he had come while pulling his phone out of his belt holster. He knew they were short-handed over the holidays, but hopefully Jamie would find someone to meet him at DeGroots'. In the meantime, he'd stop over at the Johnson place to notify them of the body found yesterday, and see if Jean Johnson knew anything about the missing horses. There had to be a connection. If he was lucky, Harvey Junior would not be there. He didn't need a protective spouse helping the interrogation.

Al rang the front doorbell and waited. A teenage girl in jeans and scuffed western boots opened the door and called for her mother as soon as Al identified himself. He knew the twins were named Ellie and Georgia, but he had no idea which one this was and she didn't volunteer her name. He asked if he could speak to Jean Johnson. The daughter disappeared into the hallway. Al stood waiting inside the front door for several minutes. He could hear them talking but couldn't make out any words. Finally, a short, slightly overweight woman who appeared to be in her late forties walked into the room. She was pulling her bleached-blond hair back into a ponytail and looked like she had just awakened. Her face was the face of a beauty queen except for the dark circles and bags under her eyes. She wore a red turtleneck and red plaid flannel pajama bottoms. Her feet were bare. Her neck disappeared and Al came to realize how the term "turtleneck" originated. She asked Al if he'd like to sit down motioning toward the clean but old-fashioned floral sofa. He started to remove his boots, but she waved it off.

"Don't worry, Sheriff, the carpet needs cleaning anyway." She smiled, but Al detected nervousness in her. The carpet looked spotless to him.

He chose the chair closest to the door. Mrs. Johnson chose the sofa.

"I'm not the sheriff, Mrs. Johnson. I'm Deputy Al Lawson. I'm just following up on your missing horses, and..." he paused not knowing what to say about the body found on the DeGroot farm yesterday. "You are aware that a body was found yesterday in your neighbor's cornfield?"

"Of course I am. Harvey told me last night. And it was on the news. We called the coroner's office but no one answered. It was late, but we needed to know if it was Harvey's dad. We called again this morning. The only thing," she took a breath, "all the woman would tell us is that an autopsy is scheduled for Monday. Do you know anything? I, I, I" she stuttered, "I would think we'd be the first ones to be notified." She was getting more agitated and her voice rose to near shrieking. The daughter came into the room and sat down on the sofa next to her mother. "I mean he's been missing since June and... ." She shook her head and looked at Al. "Why did you come here if you don't know whose body it is?"

"I hoped you could answer some questions, Mrs. Johnson. No one wants to upset you and your family unnecessarily," he paused not knowing how much to reveal. "It's possible dental records or DNA will be needed to confirm the identity. I can tell you that there was no ID on the body. So it could take days, Mrs.

Johnson. In the meantime, I hoped you could answer some questions about why, or how, your horses ended up in a barn on the DeGroot property. Can you shed any light on that?"

"No. Didn't Harvey tell you we were as shocked as anybody to know the DeGroots stole our horses?"

"Yes, but according to my notes, you and the girls were here all day the day they went missing. Did you see or hear anything?" Jean Johnson stared at the deputy for what seemed like an hour, but he was taking a page from Bobby's book, and knew that silence is often the best interrogation technique. Then, Jean Johnson began to cry, quietly at first, but soon grew to what could only be described as a keening. Her daughter immediately sat closer and put her arms around her mother.

"Mom, just tell the deputy what you told me last night. You were only trying to save our horses. It's not like it's a big crime. Mom, you'll feel better. Please tell him."

Al sat forward in his chair. *What was happening*?

"I'd like to call my husband. I haven't been well, and I need him here."

"I'll call him, Mom. But, you're fine." She looked at Al. "Mom's been seeing a doctor since Grandpa disappeared. It's been really hard on her, but I know she'll feel better if she tells you what happened. Mother, just tell the deputy what you did." she begged. "I'll call Dad." She pulled a cell phone out of her jeans pocket and punched in a number as she got up and walked out of the room.

"Ellie, can you get me some tissues, too?" The girl stood up and walked down the hallway. She returned immediately with a box of tissues and handed it to her mother. Al didn't know what to say. He decided he should just wait silently. Ellie left the room. He could hear her on her phone trying to get in touch with Harvey Junior. He hoped Mrs. Johnson would talk to him before Junior showed up.

"Ma'am?" Jean looked up at him. She shrugged her shoulders as though giving up.

"I had to do something," she began. "Harvey was going to ship those horses to Canada to be slaughtered. The girls' horses. For horsemeat." She gestured with her hands and stood up. "My own husband was going to sell those beautiful horses to be slaughtered." She paced back and forth in front of him. "He said we need the money, but we don't. We don't need it that bad anyway. What could I do?" She looked at Al pleading. "What choice did I have? I wasn't going to let him do that." Her daughter came back into the room and asked her mother to try to calm herself. They both sat back down on the sofa and Mrs. DeGroot dropped her head into her hands. Al gave her a minute to compose herself before asking her what seemed incredulous to him.

"Ma'am, are you telling me you took those horses to the DeGroot farm yourself? You were going to keep them there indefinitely?"

"No. No. Hannah DeGroot helped me." Al leaned forward. "We used our horse trailer. It was snowing hard, so I knew the tracks would be covered up. Hannah has friends in Montana who were going to come yesterday and take the horses," she took a deep breath, "to Montana where they'd be safe. All except their old nag. It wouldn't have survived a long trip like that."

"Hannah DeGroot helped you take your own horses to her farm, and then she was going to have them taken to Montana? Wouldn't your girls be heartbroken to have their horses taken out of state never to be seen again?"

She looked at Deputy Lawson. Then, at her daughter, who had begun to cry.

"They'd have been safe. They wouldn't be slaughtered anyway. I would have told the girls, eventually. Maybe we could have driven out there to see them." She looked at her daughter, hoping for some sort of confirmation that this was an excellent plan, but Ellie only shook her head back and forth. "And the good thing was those horses helped Hannah's mother. Edith Edna loved those horses and spent hours every day with them, even mucking out the barn."

Al heard the crunch of tires on packed snow and looked out the large picture window. Harvey Junior was jumping out the door of his pickup truck and bolting toward the house. The back door slammed open and a red-faced man emerged in the living room. Al stood.

"What's this all about?" Junior looked straight at Al, ignoring his wife and daughter.

Al held out his hand in greeting. Junior motioned it away. Al did his best to calmly explain what had just transpired. He expected Junior to deny it all, but was surprised when he sat down beside his wife and hugged her.

"It's okay, Jeannie. It's okay. It's all gonna be okay." Then he looked over at his daughter and asked her to take her mother to her bedroom to get some rest. "Maybe get her a cup of tea?" The younger woman helped her mother to her feet. Jean Johnson turned toward her husband.

"I'm sorry, Baby. I just didn't want you sending the horses away."

"Ellie, take her to our room and stay with her." He waited until we heard a door close behind them. "What's gonna happen now, Deputy? My wife isn't well. No one knows this, but she's been under psychiatric care since Dad disappeared. She isn't coping. She's—I don't know." He threw up his hands. "It's been hard on all of us. You know?"

"I'm sure it has, Mr. Johnson, but your wife said you were going to sell those horses for slaughter. Is that true?"

"No, that's not true. I would never do that. I don't know where she got that idea even. Maybe Hannah DeGroot put that idea into her head. Just for the record, I had no idea Jean and Hannah took those horses to DeGroots'. You need to talk to Hannah DeGroot. She and Jean were close friends years ago. Then, Hannah moved away. This might all have been Hannah's idea."

"You never said you were going to sell the horses?"

"No."

"You don't need the money selling the horses would bring in?"

"No. Things are a little tight right now, but we don't need money that bad. Can I ask about the body you found yesterday?"

"Sure, but we don't know anything yet."

"I understand, but can I see the body? I might recognize something. The clothes? Was he wearing a watch or ring? I'd know Dad's watch and ring."

"Sure. Let me call the coroner's office and we'll set up a time today, if possible. I can't make any promises though. We wanted to save you that trauma, to be honest. You can imagine there isn't much to see after all this time, and we don't like to put relatives through that if we don't have to." Junior nodded knowingly. Al pulled his stocking cap down over his shaved head and took a few steps toward the door. He turned back to Junior and told him he was sorry to have caused Mrs. Johnson distress, and that he'd get back to him as soon as he could about viewing the body. "Just one more question, if you don't mind," Al added.

"Shoot."

"You will receive quite a large inheritance from your father's estate, if your father is, in fact, deceased. Is that correct?"

Harvey Junior faked a laugh. "Depends on what you mean by large, I guess. Dad was a gambler. Gambled away any inheritance other than that house over there. Not sure what it's worth. So, no, I didn't kill my dad for an inheritance if that's what you're thinking."

"Sorry, sir. Had to ask. I'll get back to you later today about seeing the body." Al thanked him and left.

It had seemed he was in the Johnson living room for hours, but looking at his watch, Al saw he'd only been inside for twenty minutes. Jamie had left a message on his cell phone saying Deputy Lovig would join him at the DeGroot farm about nine o'clock after checking out a report of vandalism at the school. O nine hundred, Al thought. The morning was off to a good start. He felt sorry for the Johnsons, but he was also grateful for the information he'd just learned. Heading back to the DeGroot farm, he wondered if Hannah would admit to helping Jean Johnson move those horses.

As Al pulled off the country road into the DeGroots' long snow-covered lane, he replayed Junior and Jean Johnson's conversations and Jean's confession in his head. *It was a confession, but was it a crime*? Al didn't have to figure that out now. The Johnsons weren't going anywhere, although there was still the possibility that one of them killed Harvey Senior, especially if there were financial problems. Was Junior angry enough at his father for gambling away his and his siblings' inheritance to kill him in a fit of rage? Possible. He braked to a stop near DeGroots' house and with the engine still running, pulled his notebook and ballpoint pen out of his vest pocket and began to write. The whole thing sounded crazy, but he believed both Johnsons were telling the truth.

A sudden loud bang on his window startled him.

Chapter 22

It was close to eleven when I picked up Pippi at Al's house. She was wearing jeans tucked into her boots and a white down-filled jacket. She carried her cell phone in her hands. No purse. The temperature had dipped into the twenties, and Pippi's teeth chattered. "Where are your mittens?" I asked as I backed down the driveway and headed into Monroe. She gave me a dirty look to let me know she was an adult and could take care of herself. Then, she pulled them out of her pockets. We were soon on the county road leading to DeGroot's farm. It was sunny but windy, and snow blew across the road in front of us.

"Thanks, Mom. I can't imagine why Al wouldn't answer his cell phone. He never lets it run down."

"Doesn't he have a two-way radio in his Jeep? If he had a problem, he could still get in touch with headquarters, Pippi. I don't think you should be worried about him, but if he's not at DeGroots', we can call the office and find out where he is. Right?"

"Sure. I hope he's at DeGroots' though." She took a deep breath and settled back into the seat just as my cell phone started to ring. I still wasn't used to that sound and looked over at Pippi.

"It's your phone, Mom. Want me to get it for you?" she asked as she reached into my purse and pulled it out. She looked at it and said, "It's your lover boy. Want me to answer?"

"No." Then, I hesitated. "Yes, but do *not* tell him where we are going," I hissed. She looked at me like I was deranged.

"Ah, hi Sheriff. Mom's right here but she's driving, so I answered. How's Vegas?"

"Pippi, good to hear your voice. I'd say Las Vegas is starting to get old. Can your mother pull over and talk for a minute, or are you two on a big shopping excursion?"

"Ah, yes, a big shopping excursion, Sheriff." Pippi was staring at me strangely and trying to get me to take the phone from her. "Here, Mom can tell you all about it," and she handed me the phone.

"Bobby. Hi. I've missed you. How are you? How are Scott and Tennille and the baby?"

"It's a long story, Red. I miss you, too. That's why I'm calling. I think I'm flying home tomorrow. The kids are settled in for the time being at Tennille's mother's place, and Scottie has a new job starting next week. I'll tell you all about it when I see you, but I wanted to know how you've been doing and what you've been doing." I didn't answer. I didn't know what to say, and I was concentrating on navigating a snow-drifted hilly road. "You're driving, Mary Jo. I shouldn't be bothering you."

"No, Bobby, that's okay. The road isn't very good though."

"Are you headed into Des Moines?"

"No, we're…" I couldn't finish. Pippi had told him we were on a shopping trip, and that would mean Des Moines, and that would mean a snow-cleared highway. I didn't want to lie to Bobby. "We're just running some errands actually, but I did want to tell you something Lola told me." Then, it dawned on me. "Oh, my gosh!" I suddenly remembered Bobby didn't know about Joe's heart attack yet. I slowed down and pulled into DeGroots' long lane.

"What? What's wrong?"

"Oh, my gosh, Bobby. Joe had a heart attack last night, and he's in the hospital. They operated on him in the middle of the night. He had quadruple bypass surgery." By this time, the DeGroots' mint green house was in sight and so was Al's Jeep in their drive. "Oh good." I said without thinking.

"What's good about that? It doesn't sound good at all, Mary Jo. Quadruple bypass surgery at Joe's age cannot be good."

"No, I didn't mean that. I meant it's good we're at our destination now."

"Okay. But, can you tell me more about Joe? How he's doing. How is Noni taking it?"

I pulled up directly behind Al's Jeep and put my car in park, leaving the engine running so we wouldn't freeze. Pippi jumped out and looked into Al's car window and then opened his driver's door. From where I sat, I could see the car was empty. She looked back at me and shrugged her shoulders, then headed toward the house. Two cats basked in the sun on the cement step out of the wind.

Stop, Pippi! Wait for me.

"Bobby, I need to go, but Joe seems to be doing okay. I saw him this morning, and he talked a little. He's in good hands at the hospital, you know? Noni is shaken, but her daughter is on her way here to stay with her. I can't tell you much more than that right now. Are you really coming home tomorrow?"

I watched as Pippi knocked on the front door.

"Yes, I don't have my ticket yet, but it's my plan. Then, I might have to come out again in a couple of weeks, but," he paused. "I miss you, Mary Jo. I miss talking with you. I have so much I want to tell you."

"Me, too, Bobby. Oh, there's one thing I wanted to tell you earlier. Lola told me Harvey Johnson was a heavy gambler, and she thinks he gambled away all his money. Did you know that?"

Now, Pippi looked back at me and motioned with her arm for me to come.

"No, no I didn't. Did you tell Al?"

"Well, no, we're trying to find Al right now. I mean Pippi is trying to find Al. I mean he wasn't picking up his phone all morning and she got worried, and I decided to just drive her out here to DeGroots' to see if he's still here, and he is. At least his Jeep is in their driveway." I heard Bobby's intake of breath, and could imagine him combing his fingers through his hair in aggravation.

"Mary Jo, get out of there now. I mean it. Get Pippi and get out. You're basically at a crime scene. I'll get a hold of Al or somebody and get back to you. Okay?" I looked back at the front door and Pippi was no longer standing there. I looked around the yard, but didn't see her or anyone. I got out of my car still holding my phone. The wind whistling through ice-covered trees was the only sound I heard. I turned around in a circle frantically looking for Pippi. A voice in my head said, "A game of cat and mouse is afoot." *Did Holmes say that, or was it Watson*? I realized I was scared, but I didn't want Bobby to know.

"I've got to go, Bobby. I don't see Pippi. I think she might be in the house." A chill ran through my body.

"Get back into your car, Mary Jo, and hang up. I'll call headquarters and send someone out there. Just stay in your car until a deputy gets there." I told Bobby I would. Wasn't sure I could keep that promise. Surely, Pippi and Al would come walking out that front door. Any minute now—laughing about Al letting his phone's battery run out of juice—any minute.

Chapter 23

Al flinched and jerked his head up to see what had made the sudden explosion outside his car. A man he'd never seen before pointed a twelve-gauge shotgun at the steamed-over car window. He noted the stranger's gray beard and camouflage cap and jacket. The guy struck the window again with the gun. Again, Al flinched. A smoldering cigarette butt protruded between the man's lips, hidden by a heavy mustache and beard. His eyebrows were dark and bushy. *Vince DeGroot, no doubt.* Al tried to remember everything he'd heard about DeGroot, but it escaped him. He forced himself to remain calm. *No reason to panic. The man looked like one of the Duck Dynasty guys—the old one.* Looks aren't everything, Al reasoned, hopefully.

Al lowered his window. The man backed up and told Al to get out. Al's instinct was to reach to his shoulder for his two-way radio and call for help, but it was buried under his down jacket. *How quick could this old guy be with the trigger? Better to wait him out and see.*

"Get out!" The old man barked. "Give me that cell phone." Al nervously bit his lip and tasted blood. He reluctantly opened the car door and slowly stepped out handing over the phone. Duck Dynasty tossed it across the yard. Al watched in despair as it sank into a snow bank. Get a grip, he thought. I still have my two-way. I still have Lovig on his way, and I don't know that this guy is a real threat or just a bag of wind or maybe just a scared old man. See what you can find out, Bobby would advise.

"Mr. DeGroot. That's you, isn't it?" The man didn't respond. "I'm not here to cause any trouble. I just want to ask your daughter a few questions."

The man lowered the gun but remained silent. He was very thin. And he was old. He can't be too strong or too quick, reasoned Al. "Is Hannah home? Can we go inside?"

Al stamped his feet and acted cold. He had begun to worry about Hannah and her mother. *Where was Lovig anyway? He should have been here by now.* Al forced himself not to look down the lane. He didn't want DeGroot to know another deputy was on his way. The man seemed on edge, and Al didn't want him to feel trapped. Trapped people did things they would not ordinarily do.

"Whatta ya wanta talk ta Hannah about?"

"The horses, sir." Al suspected a little deference wouldn't hurt. "I found out from Jean Johnson that Hannah was the one who brought those horses over here. I want Hannah to confirm that. Did you know about that?"

"None of your business what I know and what I don't know."

He took the burned-down cigarette out of his mouth and flicked it into the snow. Blowing smoke over his shoulder, he relaxed his hold on the gun. "Go on," he ordered motioning Al toward the front door.

Once inside, Al was relieved to see both Hannah and her mother sitting on the sofa. They didn't appear to be harmed in any way, although Hannah looked apprehensive, if not downright scared.

"Hannah, get a kitchen chair in here, and get me some rope. Take the clothesline down if you have to."

"Daddy, no. What're you gonna do? Don't do this. Mom and I, we're fine." She put her arm around her mother's shoulders and took a deep breath. "Daddy, this is Deputy Lawson and he's been good to us. Everyone has been good to us. Just let him go. You can leave and no one will come looking for you." She begged.

"Dammit, Hannah. Do what I say. Yer not fine. They're gonna arrest yer mother for killing Johnson. Do you want that?" he yelled. "They'll put you in jail, too, for bein' an accessory to the crime. Yer smart enough to know that, aren't ya?" Hannah began to cry. Vince DeGroot breathed out in disgust or something and left the room. Within seconds, he came back with a kitchen chair. "Sit down, dammit," he motioned to Al.

Al debated sitting in the chair, but DeGroot was already yanking the venetian blinds and cords off the front window. Being tied to a chair with those cords wouldn't be the worst thing that could happen, but Al couldn't see any good coming from it. Even if Deputy Lovig arrived soon, Al being tied up would just put Lovig in danger, too. Al tried to stall for time.

"You're not planning on killing me, are you? That would be a mistake, Mr. DeGroot. Ah, Vince, can you tell me what you meant when you said they'd arrest your wife for killing Johnson?"

"She killed him. It was a damn accident, though. But who's gonna believe us?"

DeGroot now stood holding several cords from the blinds. Enough to tie up several people, Al thought.

"An accident?" Al wanted to hear more. "Accidents happen. Especially on farms. Can you tell me about it? How it happened?" Hannah appeared to come to life. She jumped up off the sofa. She was shaking all over and still crying.

"I'll tell you what you want to know. This all has to come to an end."

"No, Hannah. I'm warnin' you. You'll both go to jail. Ya want that? Yer mother to rot away in a jail cell?"

"Daddy, no, but Mom's sick. They won't put her in jail. They might get help for her. Please, let me tell him what happened. Don't do anything stupid. Please." Her father drew a deep breath.

"Okay, but I'm not lettin' him take yer mother away. Do ya hear me?"

"Calm down, Daddy. I don't care anymore. I can't go on like this. You deserted us, Daddy." She stood up and faced her father.

"Hannah, I put up with yer mother's craziness for as long as I could. I'm sorry I left, but I jist couldn't take it no more. I threw in the towel and beat it outta here 'cause I thought I'd be blamed fer Johnson's death. I loved yer mother, Hannah, but she ain't the same woman now. You can see that."

"Yes, Daddy. I know, but just let me tell this deputy what happened. It wasn't your fault. No one will blame you when they hear the truth. Please." Her father looked at her in defeat, but didn't say anything. Hannah looked at Al and quickly told him about last June. How she'd seen her father drag a body into their cornfield one night from the direction of the Johnson farm. Then, she recounted what DeGroot had told her about it. While Hannah was still talking, no one noticed her mother getting up off the sofa. In an instant, Edith Edna tried to grab the gun from her husband's hands. Al saw his opportunity and made his move. He tackled DeGroot from behind and both of them fell down, the shotgun sliding across the wood floor. He had control of Vince DeGroot and was reaching for the handcuffs on his utility belt when a pain seared through the side of his head. Al's last thought before he collapsed on top of DeGroot was of Pippi.

"What the?" moaned DeGroot as he pulled himself out from under Al. Hannah stood frozen in place as her mother picked up the shotgun. Then, Hannah heard a noise in the hallway and watched as her father fell to the ground holding a bloody hand to his chest. This time, Vince DeGroot was silenced. He tried once to get up before he collapsed.

Hannah looked all around the room to see where the two pops came from. Were they gunshots? Who fired them? From where? Then she acted. She dropped to her knees and put her fingers on Al's neck checking for a pulse. She didn't feel anything, but she was no nurse she thought to herself. Then, she looked at her father and knew he was gone. He was dead, and she felt an overwhelming sadness and sense of loss. What had just transpired was beyond her comprehension. She only knew someone had been in the hallway and that someone must have shot both the deputy and her father.

A knock on the front door made Hannah's heart stop. Her eyes darted to her father, and then to her mother. But, her mother had disappeared. "Shit," Hannah muttered as she heard the back door slam shut. She felt panic rise from her stomach to her head and back down to her wobbly knees. Was that the killer? Was it her mother? Maybe the killer is using her mother as a hostage? Her hands shook uncontrollably as she stepped over to the front window and peeked out. A young woman stood on the step holding the storm door open. Hannah's heart skipped a beat as her eyes flitted to the car parked next to the deputy's SUV. Hannah recognized the woman in the driver's seat as a friend of Sheriff Hanley. The woman who'd been here when Johnson's body was found in the cornfield. *This was it then. This is how it is going to end.* A calm came over her. Then, Hannah opened the front door and pulled Pippi inside.

"You have a cell phone?" Hannah pleaded.

"Well, sure, but why?" Then, Pippi, following Hannah's turning head, saw Al face down on the living room floor with blood seeping out of his forehead. She ran to him screaming his name over and over. "Oh my God. Oh my God." She saw the wound on the side of his head above his ear. "Al, baby, can you hear me?” She fumbled for her cell phone in her jacket pocket and dialed 911.

Chapter 24

"Well, this is ridiculous," I thought. "Pippi is inside the house of a murder suspect, and Al, my future son-in-law, is missing. I won't leave my daughter alone in there. Even if I wanted to leave, I can't leave." I was now talking aloud to myself. I got out of the car, with the door standing open wondering what to do, when I heard a car engine. I spun around as a Jasper County sheriff's car pulled up behind me. A uniformed deputy got out of his car and introduced himself as Mike Lovig.

"You must be Mary Jo McGee. Deputy Lovig," he said nodding my way. "The sheriff called and asked for all available units to get out here. Any idea what's going on inside? Any idea where Deputy Lawson is?" I quickly told him all I knew and that I was worried about both Al and Pippi. When I told him that Al had not answered his cell phone all morning, Deputy Lovig frowned. "Doesn't sound like Deputy Lawson, does it?" Lovig looked around the yard and at the sheds. He pulled his gun from his holster. "Get inside your car, Mrs. McGee, and get down out of sight."

Reluctantly, I obeyed the officer although *out of sight* was a term I had difficulty defining. I was peeking over the steering wheel when I saw the front door open and Pippi run out directly into the body of Deputy Lovig.

"Help. Please help. It's Al."

I couldn't hear what Pippi was shouting at Deputy Lovig, but I saw the scared look on her face. I got out of my car as fast as I could and ran to her. I smelled something evil in the air and looked around me. Something black caught my eye as it ran behind the old shed in back.

"Mom, Al's hurt." She grabbed my shoulder and pulled me toward the house. "He's been shot. I called 911, but it'll be forever before they get here. He's bleeding, but he's alive."

Deputy Lovig asked Pippi who was still in the house. "No one except a dead man and Hannah DeGroot."

"Do you know if she's armed?"

"No, Hannah doesn't have a gun. Hurry. Al is bleeding. Hannah's helping him."

"I need you both to wait out here for a minute. I'll come get you if it's safe." Reluctantly, we obeyed. True to his word, Deputy Lovig came back shortly and let us in. We all raced to Al, where Hannah DeGroot knelt by his side, pressing a towel against his head wound. A pool of blood stained the wooden floor. Tears stung my eyes. I hadn't known until then how much I loved Al. He was the son I never had. He was the future husband of my youngest daughter. He was the future father of my grandchildren. Now, I saw that future bleeding out onto an old wooden floor.

I quickly told Lovig I saw someone or something running around the shed in back of the house.

Deputy Lovig knew as soon as he saw both Al's and DeGroot's wounds, they had come from a gun and since he hadn't heard any shots, he knew the gun had a silencer. He also knew from the cold air rushing in from the hallway, that a door or window was open in the house. He drew his Smith & Wesson and immediately called for backup. Not wanting to wait, he started down the hallway and out the back door of the farmhouse. It was easy to track someone's footprints in fresh snow. The footprints appeared small in size. Possibly a child's or a woman's, he thought, but a child or a woman with a gun was just as dangerous as anybody large. He followed the tracks which led directly to the shed, but not to the door. The tracks went to the side. Deputy Lovig stuck his head around the side of the shed to have a look, but jumped back out of sight when a bullet hit the wood a few feet away from where he stood. He didn't see the shooter, but knew he had the advantage. First, he had backup arriving soon, and second, there was virtually no place the shooter could run or hide. Unless he or she could get into the shed from the other end and sneak up on him from inside. Lovig looked back at the house. He guessed maybe ten minutes had passed since he'd left the house. Then, he heard the siren. He saw the ambulance arrive, but couldn't take the time to think about Al.

While two EMTs took care of Al, I decided to look out the back door toward that shed. I was worried about Deputy Lovig and curious about the person or thing I'd seen. I stepped out on the concrete step. The silence was deafening at first, and then I saw something that chilled me to the bone. It was a person dressed all in black including a black hood. The person held what looked like a gun out in front as he or she crept slowly along the side of the shed. Deputy Lovig had his back turned and was heading toward the back of the shed. I wanted to scream a warning at him, but nothing came out of my mouth. Time seemed to stand still as I starting walking, then running toward the shed. I may have waved my arms and yelled at the deputy. I don't remember, but I do remember him turning around and yelling at me to go back. In that moment, the person in black aimed what turned out to be a .22 caliber pistol at me and fired, missing me by a long shot, or so I've been told. In those few seconds, Lovig ran around the corner of the shed and threw the person to the ground. He ripped off the hood. I didn't recognize the person, but it appeared to be a woman. Lovig was putting handcuffs on her as two other officers ran from the house and joined him. They asked if I was okay, and other than being a little shaken, I felt fine. Worried about Al, of course, but fine. The woman seemed gleeful as she was marched to the patrol cars. She smiled at me while I stood frozen on the back stoop.

What happened next? I vaguely remember the sound of sirens and following an ambulance to the hospital in Newtown. Sitting in a waiting room with Pippi. Knowing Al was taken into surgery as soon as the ambulance arrived. I remember talking with Cara and then with Ann on the phone. Thinking about a different waiting room in a different hospital a couple of nights ago with Noni. Now, waiting for word from Al's surgeon. Please, please, please, let Al be all right. I remember Bobby calling to tell me he had landed in Des Moines and that he'd come straight to the hospital. His voice sounded strange until I realized he was crying. I also knew that Hannah's mother had been found in a shed on their property and was admitted to the same hospital we now sat in waiting for word of Al. We were told she was incoherent and agitated and nearly frozen to death when they found her snuggled in a horse blanket in the shed.

A miniature Christmas tree still sat on a coffee table in the waiting room, and I watched Pippi pick it up, turning it around and around and humming. Fa la la la la. We took turns standing by the window on the third floor watching the snow fall, but mostly we sat and waited. Suddenly, a man in a rumpled shirt and worn jeans was standing in the doorway. It was Bobby. I couldn't believe it. Relief seeped through me. I stood up but couldn't move. He came to me and wrapped his arms around me and held me tight, so tight I couldn't breathe.

"Bobby. I thought … I thought you wouldn't get here so soon. I'm not sure I was even thinking." I started to cry.

"There, there. Come here, Pippi." He opened up his arms to include Pippi. She let him hold her and me until we all stopped crying. Slowly, we disentangled ourselves. Bobby cleared his throat. "Jamie met me at the airport and drove me down, lights flashing and siren going the whole way." He looked around and ran his fingers through his hair, which had grown longer since I'd seen him. "Have you heard anything?"

"No." I answered. "The surgeon talked with us before though. He said a bullet was imbedded in Al's skull close to his optic nerve, and he hoped there would be no major damage to his eye." I tried to remember everything the surgeon said. "He said he wasn't sure they could save Al's right eye." I started to cry again.

"Okay then. We wait. Have you two eaten anything? I could get you something. Coffee, tea, hot chocolate?" And so the evening hours passed with me telling Bobby how brave Pippi was to go barging into DeGroots' house looking for Al. Bobby joked how the apple doesn't fall far from the tree, but I knew he was thinking how Pippi could have gotten hurt—how we both could have gotten hurt. Then, we decided to call Kevin and let him know what had happened to Al. I didn't want to worry Kevin, but he needed to know. It was Pippi who took the phone from my hands and told Kevin not to worry—that Al was going to be all right, and that she'd phone him in the morning when she knew more.

Over the next few hours, Bobby found out that the person in black was Bernadette Johnson, the ex-wife of the missing Harvey Johnson, Sr. She shot Al by mistake. She had been aiming at

Vince DeGroot. Why? Because Vince DeGroot had been blackmailing her for six months. Seems Vince had followed his wife, Edith Edna, over to the Johnson farm one evening last June. Edith Edna had often wandered over there to look at the horses. Most nights he'd watch as Edith Edna called each horse to her and petted them sometimes climbing inside the gated enclosure to get closer. It kept her happy and Vince didn't see any harm in letting her do it. But one night he was busy working on a piece of machinery and didn't follow her until much later. It was after dark when he walked through the pasture and reached the Johnson farm. He heard his wife moaning from inside the barn and another woman yelling at her to leave. DeGroot ran around to the entrance and peeked into the barn. Bernadette Johnson was pointing a gun at a very agitated Edith Edna DeGroot. A body lay at their feet. Vince approached slowly in disbelief, but always on the lookout for an easy buck, saw an opportunity to make some money. A damsel in distress is how he thought of Bernadette Johnson at that moment.

He put his arm around his wife calming her, and asked her if she could walk back home by herself. She nodded and left after giving the dead man at her feet one last look.

While Bobby was explaining all this to Mary Jo, she wondered about Bernadette Johnson and how a woman with an apparently good life could turn into a cold-blooded murderer. Why not just divorce her philandering husband? And now that she was caught, how she could relay the night of the murder so clearly to Bobby. She seemed to remember every detail in the conversation between her and Vince DeGroot. Bobby continued with that very conversation, or as close to the real conversation as Bernadette could repeat. Hannah DeGroot also filled in some of the details her father had told her about that fateful conversation. It went something like this:

"What happened here?" Vince asked, although he was pretty sure he knew Bernadette must have finally gotten tired of her husband's gambling and philandering and shot him.

"It was an accident, Vince. He must have shot himself."

"Sure. And that's why you're holding the gun?" he slowly scratched his shaggy beard like he was trying to find a solution to climate change.

Bernadette Johnson soon figured out she couldn't fool her neighbor, and she also figured he might be able to help her dispose of the body for a couple hundred dollars. Vince bargained for a lot more than a couple hundred, and offered to dispose of the body for her for another thousand.

I was so engrossed in Bobby's relaying of the murder, we didn't notice the surgeon enter the room. He cleared his throat and told us in a quiet, monotone voice that the surgery went well and that Al would be in recovery for about another hour and then taken to a room on the third floor. Pippi asked if she could see him and the doctor kindly offered to take us all to the recovery room.

We both looked at Pippi. She looked exhausted but still had something about her that I can only describe as hope and love and optimism.

"Mary Jo, let's leave Pippi to be alone with Al while we just head home."

"Home, Bobby?"

"Sure. Your home, Sweetie. I've got my bag with me. I'll tell you all the rest on the way."

So, we hugged Pippi good-bye and gathered up our coats. Bobby pulled his knit cap down over his ears as we left the warmth of the hospital and headed to the parking lot. Fresh snow had fallen and someone, or more than one, had made snow angels on the lawn. I took this as a good omen. I kicked my boots gently on the side of the car door to knock off the snow as I got into Bobby's car. The car was cold, and we sat waiting for it to warm up before pulling out. Plows and sanders were out on the lonely middle-of-the-night streets. I looked over at Bobby and knew he was thinking the same thing I was. Would Al be okay? Was he really out of the woods? I told Bobby we should be optimistic, and then I asked the other question that was bugging me.

"But, why did Bernadette kill Vince DeGroot today?" I asked.

"He got greedy. Blackmailers often get greedy, and it often results in their sudden death. Bernadette was running out of cash, too. Let's just say she knew how to spend it. But, it was more than that, I think. She's what we call a parasite. She'll go along with any atrocity, so long as her own security is assured. Bernadette Johnson saw herself as a victim who had no choice other than to kill her husband. Then, she blamed Vince DeGroot for blackmailing her and so had no choice other than to kill him."

"Bobby, when I was at the DeGroots' the day Harvey Johnson's body was found, Hannah kept saying he looks human, or something like that. I wonder what she meant."

"Well, Harvey Johnson wasn't a saint by any means, and I don't think Bernadette's life with him was easy. Hannah DeGroot evidently told one of the deputies that Harvey Johnson hit both her and her mother one night when they were just visiting the horses, and threatened them with a gun if they didn't leave. Anyway, when Bernadette Johnson stopped sending DeGroot money, he decided to come back to force her hand. She wasn't about to pay him anymore, so killing him was her solution."

We were all the way home before I remembered I left my car at the hospital but Bobby said we'd get it in the morning. I let Archie out although he was excited to see Bobby and wanted back inside right away. We made tea and sat at the kitchen table winding down from the day's emotional ride. I wanted to hear more about Bobby's time in Las Vegas, but it could wait. We got ready for bed. It felt good to have Bobby back. We said how much we had missed each other as we climbed into bed. Bobby looked more than just tired as he sneezed and pulled the quilt up over us.

"Bobby?"

"Hmmm?"

"Did you ever find out why Hannah didn't want her corn picked? Surely, she didn't know Harvey Johnson's body was out there."

"Well, yes, she did know. She saw her dad drag the body into the cornfield and confronted him. He told her about Bernadette killing her husband, and was afraid it could be blamed on Edith Edna or himself. He said he was going to leave. He thought by the time the body was discovered, he'd be long gone, and he hoped Edith Edna wouldn't be a suspect because of her illness."

"Ahhh. Not to change the subject, but Scott is lucky to have you for a father," I mumbled half asleep already.

"Do you really think so?" He searched my face, his eyes sad. His eyes closed before I could answer, so I wrapped him in my arms and fell asleep thinking that in the morning we'd drive separately to the hospital to see Al. That way Bobby could check in at the sheriff's office, and I could check on Noni and Joe. Life goes on. Maybe the winter solstice did bring about a new beginning.

Chapter 25

I woke to the sound of Bobby taking a shower and rolled over to the middle of the bed before I remembered the events of the previous day. I scrambled out of bed at the same time the phone rang. It was Pippi telling me Al was awake and hungry.

"He has a huge bandage on his head that covers his eye, but he's talking to me. He doesn't remember being shot or what led up to it, but he remembers everything else. The nurse said the surgeon will be in around ten to see him. Mom, when can you get here?"

I looked around the bedroom thinking of what to wear. Bobby came out of the bathroom and whispered that Archie was outside already and a kettle of hot tea was waiting for me. I nodded gratefully and told Pippi we'd both be there right away if she needed us.

"No. No. Mom, it's not that urgent. I was just wondering. We're fine here, but if you're coming, could you bring me a toothbrush?"

I assured her I could do that, but if it was okay, I'd really like to check on Joe and Noni first. I knew I could borrow Noni's car since she wouldn't be needing it. Poppi agreed I should do that and told me to give them her love. So, by the time I was dressed, Bobby had left for the office and said he'd meet me at the Newtown hospital as soon as he could get away. I called Kevin and gave him an update on Al's condition, and asked if he could open up the shop this morning. Then, I gave Archie a hug and headed to Holland's hospital to see Joe.

Miracles do happen. Joe was sitting in a chair and gave me a big smile as I walked in. Noni and their daughter were sitting on the bed and all were waiting for a nurse who was going to take Joe for a short walk in the corridor. We all had a good visit, and I was beyond happy to see Joe looking so well, but when the nurse came in for the walk, I decided it take my exit and head for Newtown to see Al and Pippi.

"I haven't had a chance to tell anyone about some good news I received. The day I visited Killian at Anamosa, he told me he wants to deed the Book Nook to me."

"What? Mom, that's wonderful. He wants to just give it to you? Can he do that?" asked Pippi.

"I think so. He owns it. He owns the whole building. I'd like to give him something though. I also want to think about expanding the shop to include the second floor, or," I paused thinking, "should I rent out the second floor to someone? There's a lot to think about. Oh! That reminds me, Al, your cousin, Lola, came up with the perfect new name for the Book Nook."

"Lola did? Well, let's hear it."

"Boek Winkel. Maybe Der Boek Winkel? We thought it should be a Dutch name and that is Dutch for book store. Voila."

Amid the oohs and aahs, Bobby interrupted.

"I have some good news, too, and it's along that same line, Red." We all quieted down and waited for him to continue.

"Killian Nolan is going to be released from prison with time served provided he is willing to move back to Ireland, which he says he is. Governor Hughly pardoned Killian just this morning. I got a courtesy call from the warden at Anamosa just as I pulled into the parking lot."

We all screamed and jumped up and down. I threw my arms around Bobby and felt tears flood my eyes. I wiped them away and watched Pippi sit down on the bed next to Al. Bobby went on to explain that since Killian was born in Ireland and had never become a U.S. citizen, he would be free to move back to Ireland even though he was considered a felon. I was already dreaming of a trip to Ireland to visit Killian. I'd always wanted to visit there anyway. Home of my ancestors. What a day, I thought. *What a week.*

"I never thought we'd be spending New Year's Day together," I said as I stood at the kitchen sink peeling apples for Al's favorite dessert, apple pie, which I intended to deliver to him in his hospital bed first thing in the morning. Although Al's eye was still bandaged heavily, the surgeon was fairly confident there was no damage to his optic nerve, and his appetite was definitely back.

"Oh, I had it all planned that I'd be back to take you somewhere special. Being with you is special enough, but if you'd like to go somewhere like a movie or dinner, I'd take you, Red. Anywhere you want," Bobby said as he came up behind me, lifted the hair off the back of my neck and softly kissed my neck.

"Paris even?"

"Do you want to go to Paris?" He sniffed my ears and nuzzled his face into my hair.

"Mmm, someday, maybe."

"Paris it is." He turned me around toward him and smoothed the hair out of my eyes and kissed me. "Would you like to dance?" he whispered.

"Dance?" I wasn't sure I'd heard him correctly.

He placed my wet hands around his neck, drew me close to him, and started singing softly. "When I want you, in my arms, when I want you, with all your charms, whenever I want you, all I have to do is dream, dream, dream." We twirled around the kitchen floor to our favorite Everly Brothers song playing on the radio. It felt so good to have Bobby's arms around me. I breathed in his scent and cuddled into his neck.

"Now, what's this about you having a date with some professor from Central while I was gone?"

I froze. How did he know about that? Who told him?

"Who told you that?"

"Oh no, Red," he laughed. "You don't get to question me. I promised I wouldn't tell. Now, are you going to tell me about it, or do I have to put on my detective hat?" He spun me around the kitchen table again, and since he seemed to think it all quite funny, I decided to confess.

"It really wasn't a date. It was just," I paused, "just a guy, well, a guy who came into the shop and bought some books, and I thought he liked reading books as much as I do and, well, really, what I thought was that you were choosing Las Vegas over me, or maybe choosing Scott over me, and I felt I was certainly free to go out with someone if I want to, because, um," I came to a slow stop. We stopped dancing.

"Mary Jo," he hugged me tighter. Then, he kissed me. A kiss that wiped all thoughts from my mind. A kiss that made my stomach take flight. "I don't mind that you went out with someone. I'm glad you did because you will find that there is no one in this town or in this world who could love you as much as I do. One day, you'll believe that." He started to dance again very slowly even though the music had stopped. "I hope that day comes soon," he sighed.

"I'm pretty sure that day is here, Bobby. I missed you more than you know. And, that guy from Central? I didn't have any fun with him at all. It was actually a very boring date."

"You don't say."

Later that night, after visiting Al in the Newtown hospital with a piece of apple pie, and checking in on Joe and Noni back at Holland Regional, we returned to my house and collapsed in bed. Maybe tomorrow we could talk about how peaceful and calm Noni and Joe were in Joe's hospital room, and how efficient and loving Pippi was while taking care of Al, but for now, Bobby and I were tucked in for the night under my favorite yellow star quilt. The wind picked up and howled and rattled the windows, but I stayed warm snuggled next to Bobby. Neither Paris nor Las Vegas could possibly have anything more than I had right here.

The End

Lemon Bars
(Makes 16 to 20 bars)

These are the lemon bars Noni bakes for the Book Nook, or is it the Boek Winkel now?

½ cup butter, softened
1 cup plus 2 tablespoons flour (divided)
¼ cup powdered sugar
2 eggs, slightly beaten
1 cup granulated sugar
3 tablespoons fresh lemon juice
¼ teaspoon salt
1 teaspoon grated lemon zest

Mix together the butter, 1 cup flour, and powdered sugar. Put into an ungreased 8-inch pan and press with fingers to form an even layer of crust. Bake 15 minutes at 350 degrees. Mix eggs, granulated sugar, lemon juice, salt, remaining 2 tablespoons of flour, and grated lemon zest. Pour over the hot crust. Bake 20 minutes. Sift powdered sugar over lemon bars when cooled.

Eggs Benedict Casserole
(serves 12)

This is the recipe Mary Jo served her family and friends on Christmas Eve morning for brunch. It has several steps and it is not an easy dish to prepare, but it is worth the effort and an easy way to serve Eggs Benedict to a crowd.

For the casserole:
1 tablespoon olive oil plus more for the pan
6 English muffins, split and cut into 1-inch pieces
1 large leek, white and light green part only, cut into ¼ inch half moons
12 ounces Canadian bacon, chopped
6 large eggs
2 ½ cups whole milk
1 ½ teaspoons dry mustard
1 teaspoon dried chives
1 ½ cups heavy whipping cream
¾ teaspoon cayenne pepper
½ teaspoon each salt and pepper

Preheat oven to 425 degrees. Coat a 9x13 baking dish with oil. Place all the muffin pieces on a large rimmed baking sheet and bake until lightly golden, 12 to 15 minutes. Transfer to the oiled baking dish.

Reduce oven to 350 degrees

Heat oil in a large skillet over medium heat. Add the leeks and cook stirring occasionally for 4 minutes. Increase heat to medium-high and add the bacon and cook for 4 to 5 minutes until beginning to brown. Spoon this mixture over the muffins.

In a large bowl, whisk (or beat) the whole eggs, milk, dry mustard, chives, 1 ½ cups cream, and ½ teaspoon each of cayenne, salt, and pepper. Pour this mixture over the bacon-leek mixture and bake until casserole is puffed, golden brown and just set—about 40 to 45 minutes.

For the sauce:
Shortly before the casserole is done, whisk together in a small glass bowl:

8 large egg yolks at room temperature
1 tablespoon fresh lemon juice
1 teaspoon Dijon mustard
½ cup heavy whipping cream
¼ teaspoon cayenne
½ teaspoon salt
½ cup (2 sticks) unsalted butter, melted
2 tablespoons chopped fresh chives (optional)

Place the bowl over (but not in) a saucepan of simmering water and cook, whisking constantly, until the mixture is thick enough to coat the back of a spoon (about 203 minutes). Reduce heat to low. Still whisking constantly, gradually add the melted butter. Your sauce is done. You can serve it along side the casserole and let each person pour desired amount, or you can do what Mary Jo did—pour it over the whole casserole as soon as it comes out of the oven. Garnish with fresh chives if desired.

Pippi's Sweet and Salty Pecans

Pippi's sweet and salty pecans make the perfect food gift to give friends and relatives during the holidays. They are pretty in a canning jar with ribbon, or in a plastic bag lined with tissue paper and tied with ribbon. My "real" neighbor, Sharon Huff, gave me this recipe.

1 pound pecan halves
2 tablespoons butter
½ cup sugar
1/3 cup corn syrup
1 tablespoon coarse sea salt
½ teaspoon freshly ground black pepper

Washed raw sugar for sprinkling (I had never heard of this before, but it is located in your grocery store in the baking aisle in a C&H plastic bag. The sugar is the color brown, but it is not the same as brown sugar. Don't substitute.)

Preheat oven to 325 degrees. Butter a 15x10x1 inch baking pan.

Mix nuts, butter, sugar, corn syrup, sea salt, and pepper together in a bowl. Spread out on baking pan. Bake 25 minutes stirring once or twice. Remove from oven. Sprinkle generously with the raw sugar and stir. Transfer to foil and let cool. Break apart. Good up to two weeks. Can be frozen.

Fig and Quinoa Salad
(serves 6)

Pippi inherited her mother's love of cooking and growing herbs. She also likes a healthier fare than typical holiday dishes and this salad fits the bill.

1 cup quinoa
1 ¼ cups water

Dressing:
¼ cup red wine vinegar
1 tablespoon Dijon mustard
2 dried figs, soaked in warm water at least 10 minutes
¼ cup pine nuts

Salad:
1 pint fresh figs, stems removed and quartered
2 green onions, thinly sliced
¼ cup fresh basil, chopped
2 cups arugula
1 teaspoon ground black pepper
1 pinch of salt

In a medium sauce pan combine the quinoa and water and bring to a boil. Once boiling, reduce to a simmer and cover, stirring occasionally. Cook for 15-20 minutes until the liquid is absorbed.

While the quinoa is cooking, make the dressing by combining vinegar, mustard, dried figs and ¼ cup pine nuts in a blender and blend until smooth.

Combine the quinoa, fresh figs, green onions, basil and arugula in a medium bowl and toss with the dressing. Sprinkle with salt and pepper and serve.

Easy Roasted Tomato Soup
(4 to 6 servings)

Cara loves this with grilled cheese sandwiches and her boys do, too. She usually doubles the recipe.

3 pounds tomatoes, cored
1/3 cup olive oil (divided)
6 garlic cloves, minced (Pippi had to settle for her mother's jar of minced garlic in the refrigerator)
2 tablespoons chopped, fresh thyme or 2 teaspoons dried thyme
2 cups chopped onion
¼ cup minced, fresh basil or 1 tablespoon dried basil
1 can (14 ½ ounces) chicken broth
½ cup half-and-half
Salt and pepper to taste

Place tomatoes in a roasting pan; drizzle with ¼ cup oil. Sprinkle with garlic and thyme. Bake, uncovered, at 350 degrees for one hour, turning occasionally. In a large saucepan, sauté onion in remaining oil until softened. Add roasted tomatoes and basil; cook for 5 minutes. Add broth; bring to a boil. Cook and stir for 5 minutes. Put through a sieve or food mill; return puree to pan. In a small saucepan over medium-low heat, warm half-and-half (do not boil). Stir half-and-half, salt and pepper into soup.

Chocolate-Velveeta Fudge
(Yield 6 pounds)

Mary Jo says do not be afraid to make this Velveeta fudge. You don't taste the cheese—it just makes the fudge extra creamy. Don't eat all six pounds like Mary Jo's friend, Ellen, did one year.

1 pound butter
1 pound Velveeta
4 pounds powdered sugar (sifted) Mary Jo doesn't bother to sift, and it still turns out good.
1 cup cocoa (sifted) (or not)
1 tablespoon vanilla
2 cups chopped walnuts

Melt the butter and cheese in a large pan at a low temperature on stovetop. Add remaining ingredients and stir over low heat until combined. Turn off burner if it begins to scorch. Pour into a 9x13 buttered pan and let cool.

Kara's Sugar Cookie Recipe
(makes a lot)

This is the author's real daughter-in-law's cookie recipe. It has become a family tradition to make these cutout cookies at Christmas time, and at other holidays as well; just change your cookie cutters from Santa to the Easter Bunny or a jack-o-lantern or... . We've all learned to make these over two or three days instead of one day. You'll see why.

2 cups butter (not margarine), softened
2 cups sugar
2 eggs
5 cups flour
2 teaspoon baking soda
1 teaspoon salt
2 teaspoon almond extract

Mix ingredients with electric mixer and divide the dough into 4 balls. Wrap in plastic wrap and chill for 2 hours. (This is where we take a break and chill them overnight.) Then, press each ball (one at a time) flat with a potato masher or your hands, and roll out to 1/4 inch thick. You might have to let the dough balls warm up a tad if you've had them in the refrigerator overnight. Cut out with cookie cutters. Bake at 350 degrees until light brown (8 to 10 minutes). Cool slightly and place on parchment paper, granite countertop, or whatever. This is where Mary Jo takes another break. She stores the baked cookies in a large container and waits until the next day to frost them; or, they can be frozen and frosted at a later date.

Frosting
1 ½ sticks butter (not margarine)
1 bag of powdered sugar
1 teaspoon vanilla
½ cup evaporated milk

Mix butter, powdered sugar, and vanilla. Add evaporated milk and mix. Divide frosting into small bowls if you want to add food colors to the white frosting.

Lasagna for Eight

Mary Jo served this lasagna the night before Christmas Eve – the night of the blizzard and the night she met Scott's girlfriend for the first time. She always doubles this and shares with Joe and Noni next door.

½ pound ground beef
½ pound ground Italian sausage
1 cup chopped onion
2 cloves garlic, minced
1 7½ ounce can tomatoes, cut up; or buy canned diced tomatoes
1 8-ounce can tomato sauce
1 6-ounce can tomato paste
2 teaspoons dried basil
1 teaspoon dried oregano
1 teaspoon fennel seed, crushed (optional)
½ teaspoon salt
½ teaspoon pepper
5 ounces lasagna noodles (6 noodles)
1 beaten egg
2 cups ricotta cheese
½ cup grated parmesan or romano cheese (divided)
1 tablespoon dried parsley flakes
1 8-ounce package sliced mozzarella cheese

Preheat oven to 375 degrees.

Meat Sauce: In a large saucepan cook meat, onion, and garlic till meat is brown and onion is tender. Drain fat. Stir in UNDRAINED tomatoes, tomato sauce, tomato paste, basil, oregano, fennel if desired, salt, and pepper. Bring to boiling; reduce heat. Cover and simmer for 15 minutes; stir occasionally. Meanwhile, cook lasagna noodles according to package directions. Drain.

Filling: Combine egg, ricotta, ¼ cup of the parmesan or romano cheese, and the parsley flakes.

Layer HALF of the cooked noodles in a 12x7x2-inch baking dish. Spread with HALF of the filling. Top with HALF of the meat sauce and HALF of the mozzarella cheese. Repeat layers. Sprinkle the remaining parmesan cheese on top.

Bake in a 375 degree oven for 30 to 35 minutes or till heated through. Let stand 10 minutes before serving.

Can be made ahead and frozen unbaked. Just defrost and add some time to the baking process.

Pizzelles

Bobby gave Mary Jo his Italian grandmother's recipe. You need to purchase a pizzelle maker to make these light-as-a-snowflake anise-flavored treats. The author's real friend, Michele Yannuzzi, gave these treats to the Vorbrichs every Christmas for several years before giving the author the recipe.

3 ½ cups all-purpose flour
2 tablespoons baking powder
3 eggs
1 cup sugar
½ cup butter, melted and cooled
1 teaspoon vanilla
1 teaspoon anise

Thoroughly stir together flour and baking powder.
Beat eggs till foamy; stir in sugar.
Add cooled butter, vanilla, and anise to egg mixture
Stir in flour mixture; mix well. (Hard to do by hand, easy with free-standing mixer)
Chill thoroughly.
Using a tablespoon of dough for each cookie, shape into balls.
Add ball of dough to hot pizzelle maker. Squeeze lid to close.
Bake until golden color.
Turn out on rack to cool. Sprinkle with powdered sugar.

Cheeseburger Chowder
(8 servings)

Smokey Row in Pella, Oskaloosa, and Des Moines, Iowa, makes a great cheeseburger chowder, but my recipe includes some chopped dill pickles which enhances the flavor.

½ pound ground beef
¾ cup chopped onion
¾ cup shredded carrots
¾ cup diced celery
1 teaspoon dried basil
1 teaspoon dried parsley flakes
4 tablespoons butter, divided
3 cups chicken broth
4 cups diced peeled potatoes (1 and ¾ pounds)
¼ cup all-purpose flour
2 cups (8 ounces) Velveeta pasteurized prepared cheese product
1/3 cup chopped dill pickle
1 ½ cups milk
¾ teaspoon sea salt
¼ to ½ teaspoon pepper
¼ sour cream

In a 3-quart saucepan, brown beef, drain and set aside. In the same saucepan, sauté onion, carrots, celery, basil and parsley in one tablespoon butter until vegetables are tender, about 10 minutes. Add broth, potatoes and beef; bring to a boil. Reduce heat; cover and simmer for 10-12 minutes or until potatoes are tender.

Meanwhile, in a small skillet, melt remaining butter. Add flour; cook and stir for 3-5 minutes or until bubbly. Add to soup; bring to a boil. Cook and stir for 2 minutes. Reduce heat to low. Add cheese, milk, salt, pepper and diced dill pickle; cook and stir until cheese melts. Remove from the heat; blend in sour cream. Do not boil as sour cream will curdle.

Apple Pie
(serves 8)

Mary Jo makes this pie from scratch whenever she needs to calm her nerves or to give to someone who could use some love from the kitchen. We have to assume it helped Al on his road to recovery.

Pastry:
2 cups all-purpose flour
½ teaspoon salt
2/3 cup shortening or lard
6 to 7 tablespoons cold water

In a mixing bowl, stir together the flour and salt. Cut in shortening till pieces are the size of small peas. Sprinkle one tablespoon of the water over part of mixture; gently toss with a fork. Push to side of bowl. Repeat till all flour is moistened. Divide dough in half. Form each half into a ball.

On a floured surface, flatten one ball of dough with hands. Roll dough from center to edges, forming a circle about 12 inches in diameter. Wrap pastry around rolling pin. Unroll onto a 9-inch pie plate. Ease pastry into the pie plate, being careful not to stretch pastry. Trim pastry even with rim of pie plate.

Repeat for second ball of dough and put on top of apple filling. Cut slits or poke holes in top dough so steam can be released. Flute edge.

Or, buy your dough already made and rolled out at your grocery store in the refrigerated aisle. Pillsbury and Marie Callender are both good.

Apple filling:

6 or 7 Granny Smith apples peeled and cut in wedges
1 cup sugar
1 teaspoon cinnamon
1 1/2 tablespoons butter sliced into 5 or 6 pieces

Place your apples into crust. Pour sugar over the apples. Sprinkle on cinnamon. Place butter slices around top of apples. Top with the remaining crust. Poke holes with a fork or making slits with a knife to release steam while baking. Bake at 375 degrees for 60 minutes.

About the Author

Jody Vorbrich lives with her husband in the beautiful city of Des Moines. She received her Bachelor of Science degree in Education from Drake University, and is a member of the Iowa Chapter of Sisters in Crime. This is her second novel which evolved from her love of reading and solving mysteries, and from her love of living in Iowa.